MELODY'S STONE

SUZANA JAMES

Published by Flower Mantis Press 2015

A catalogue record for this book is available from the National Library of Australia.

National Library of Australia Cataloguing-in-Publication entry:
Melody's Stone / Suzana James
1. Paranormal fiction 2. Reincarnation—Fiction
3. Soul mates—Fiction
A823.4

Book cover design and formatting services by BookCoverCafe.com

First Edition 2015
ISBN 978-0-9942106 (pbk) 978-0-9942106 (e-bk)

For my son;
who teaches me daily, the true value
of unconditional love.

STARLAH ROSE rested her hand against the grainy bark of a eucalyptus tree and stared out towards the sun setting over the distant ocean. She could barely make out the shoreline from her vantage point on the cliff's edge. Sweat coated her forehead. It had taken her an hour to climb off-trail through the national park to get to this ideal spot. She closed her eyes and sucked in a deep breath, taking in the perfumed aroma of leaves and the earthy smell of wildlife.

Opening her eyes, she drank in the sun's essences, trying to capture its final rays' warmth and glory. It momentarily filled a cold spot in her heart as it melted into the horizon. The orange-buttery splash seeped into the sea, taking with it radiance and joy. She pulled her eyes from its life-giving glow and looked around the rainforest; she had to find the perfect spot before darkness prevented movement.

She saw a bush turkey scratching and pecking at the mossy surface of a large log. Starlah smiled; cool, if it was good enough for the turkey, it would be good enough for her. Besides, its squabbling would be a soothing distraction.

She cast a final glance at the receding sun, tiptoed towards the preoccupied bird, sat down on the ground and leaned against the log's cool surface. She turned to introduce herself, but the little shit took off in a hurry.

'Whatevs,' she mumbled as she let the backpack she clutched drop from her fingers. It hit the ground with a clink. She exhaled through pursed lips, letting out a soft whistle. She was disappointed the bush turkey wasn't keen on making friends, but she was grateful its taste in forest furniture was astute. This spot would definitely do. Normally, the thought of all the dirt and bugs would steer her clear of any such endeavours, but the solitude of the bush overrode any impulse to bolt home.

Squawking chatter above caught her attention. She looked up and spotted a couple of butcherbirds. They were bickering over some sort of grub and the battle looked serious. She eyed off the trajectory of their drop zone and cringed. She shuffled over until she was out of the drop zone and left them to it.

Watching the sun and listening to the forest's chatter blessed her with a momentary distraction. But the beauty of reality is its persistent ability to slap you out of any false sense of joy or delusion: the delusion that your life is great, you are loved and tomorrow will be better. The delusion that teased her all her life with what could've been, if only she had been born to some other pair of humans who valued their kid's happiness.

She darted her eyes around the forest canopy and blinked away the burn in her eyes. She wished that she had found this area to hide out a while ago … such beauty. Oh well.

The profound tiredness washing over her demanded surrender. The battle between her heart and mind over the past few hours, weighing the pros and cons to her decision, finally dismantled her armour. There was no other way to end this pain. Her parents would never become decent human beings, and there was nobody who would miss her.

The pleading eyes of Mangy, the stray dog she occasionally fed on the way home from school, stared up at her through her mind. She felt her throat tighten. The annoying part of her brain tried desperately to dissuade her … see, maybe you shouldn't do this after all. She pulled her shoulders back. Mangy's innocent face bore into her mind. She bit her lower lip – sorry, buddy, you're on your own now.

She challenged that annoying part of her brain to come up with a single person who'd shed a tear. Daniel flashed through her mind. She wished he was still around to stick up his hand. But then again, would he even give a shit? He had walked away and left her to fend for herself. She clenched her jaw.

She accepted that her parents were scum, but she never imagined that when Daniel left he would never look back. Why hadn't he come back for her? She pinched the bridge of her nose to force back the tears. How the hell did her life get to this point?

The past seventeen years had been challenging and not pleasant, but had there ever been a time when it wasn't like that?

Was there a time when fairies and rainbows painted her heart and she was somebody's – *anybody's* – little princess?

She tried to conjure up a memory of when her heart felt full and her face knew how to smile. She shook her head; that just brought her back to Daniel. The painful vice twisted harder. She bit her lip again, hard enough to hurt.

'Whatever,' she whispered, 'doesn't matter anymore, anyway.' Her dad's spectre joined the party in her mind. She sneered, 'Ha, who's gonna be your punching bag now?'

A wave of bile inched its way up her throat, bile loaded with unexpressed hatred and rage. It had been churning and boiling and rotting away in there for years. She wondered if it would overflow and ooze out of her when she no longer had the strength to hold it in, as her body finally relaxed and took her to a place where she would be free.

Looking down at her backpack, she saw the bottle of vodka she had swiped from her dad's stash poking out of the top. Deeper down in the bag was the bottle of sleepers she had nicked from her mum. She shrugged; just add it to the list.

She grabbed the vodka and unscrewed the lid. The vapour from the bottle trickled up her nose. Her hands trembled. It had her father's imprint all over it. She closed her eyes and took a swig. The clear liquid burned down her throat and hit her stomach, sending a wave of heat through her.

'Suck it up, girly,' she chastised herself and took another big swig. 'Show Daddy who grew up just like him.'

Starlah shook her head and wiped the back of her hand across her mouth. Leaves rustled, drawing her attention. She darted her eyes around, hoping that Mangy had followed her. She hated the idea of spending her last night alone.

She held her breath, waiting for his happy, slobbery face to bounce out of the bushes and lick her face. She even had some snacks for him, just in case. She prayed and waited … but no, she was all alone for this final act.

'Where the hell are ya, Mangy?' she muttered as she pulled out a camp lantern, darting her eyes from side to side. Her skin prickled, stiffening her arm hairs to attention. The eeriness of the night-time forest symphony vibrated through her spine.

Congrats Starlah, you found your deserted hideout, all right. She grabbed the bottle of vodka again, clutching it.

She took another big swig as she stared out into the darkness, wondering what it was going to be like. Would it hurt? Would she know it was happening, or would she simply slip away when she drifted off into unconsciousness? She hoped for the latter.

The burning in her throat from the booze was lessening, and she felt her lips and nose getting numb. Her body finally gave in to the sedating effects of the alcohol. The mysterious rustling and forest residents no longer drew her attention. What did it matter anyway if a wild beast ripped her life away? It'd save her having to finish the act. Maybe that would be a better way to go.

She pictured her parents' faces and shook her head. No, she wanted them to know that she did this and they were to blame. Otherwise, what was the point of all this? She raised the bottle and saluted the sky. 'Here's to me … and to you too, Mum and Dad.'

She played out a scene in her mind when her parents found out she was gone, hoping by some miracle they would show some care factor, but no matter how hard she tried she couldn't envision them grieving. She clenched her jaw with determination. *Let's get this over with.*

She reached down into the bag and pulled out the sleepers. She took a few deep breaths. 'OK. Let's do this.' She fumbled with the lid, turning it this way and that way, but it wouldn't budge. 'Freaking childproof caps,' she yelled into the surrounding forest, her voice echoing through the trees. Leaves rustled in return.

She looked around for a decent-sized rock. She picked one up, weighing its worth. It would do. She grabbed the bottle of sleepers and placed it onto the log, aimed and then smashed the crap out of the bottle. Pieces of plastic ricocheted into her face. She rubbed her cheek and noticed a speck of blood.

The little yellow pills spilled out onto the ground and blended into the undergrowth. 'Freaking shit—shit.'

She foraged through the ground, rescuing what she could of the pills. Her hand touched something cold and scaly. She snapped back her hand, shivering, hoping it wasn't a snake. A large lizard scampered away.

'Phew,' she exhaled in relief, but her heart continued to pound. Even though she wanted out, she didn't want 'death by snakebite' on her autopsy report.

She concentrated on slowing her heart rate by closing her eyes and taking slow, deep breaths. When she felt more in control of her body, she looked down at what remained of the stash. Hm, fifteen pills mixed with a litre of vodka should be enough.

She separated them into piles of fives and grabbed the bottle of vodka, getting ready to throw down the first five.

'What are you doing?'

Starlah jumped and spun her head in the direction of the male voice. She frowned, concentrating to see the figure emerging from the trees. Her heart thumped as the intruding figure came into view. His silhouette stood to the left of her and took up a significant portion of the scenery. She figured he had to be at least six-foot two tall. His shoulders bulged through his white T-shirt, and his iridescent blue eyes pierced into her, making her skin sprout goose bumps.

'What the—who the fuck are you?' she managed to croak, still clutching the bottle of vodka.

The figure walked towards her. He seemed to give off a glow. Starlah shook her head. *Must be the booze.*

'You know, you shouldn't swear. It doesn't suit you.' He smiled at her.

'What the fu—what the hell's it got to do with you?' She glared at him, but felt her face redden. For some weird reason, she didn't want to offend the stranger. She looked him up and down. 'Do I know you?' she said, sensing something familiar about him. Or maybe just about anyone would look familiar under the influence of magic vodka.

He walked up to the log and sat down beside her. He leaned his back up against the coolness of the bark and turned his head so he looked into her mocha-brown eyes. 'Well, not exactly.'

'What the hell do you mean by that?' She stared into his eyes. Her breath got caught mid-exhale. *What's up with those eyes? Too intense. Look away,* she told herself. But she couldn't turn away; they twinkled like blue diamonds. Even though the light had diminished, they still sparkled. She leaned in and studied the silver streaks spreading out from his pupils. She had never seen anything like them.

'Not in this life, anyway.' He continued to smile.

What? She shook her head to break the spell his eyes had on her. She cleared her throat. 'Oh, you're one of those … O-K, then.' She took another swig from the bottle and avoided his eyes by staring down at the pills.

She wondered how long it was going to take her to get rid of the handsome weirdo with the freaky eyes. If someone was intensely attractive, did that make up for weirdness? She looked back at her new friend and nodded. Yeah, it sure did. He seemed to radiate beauty even though he was muscular and rugged. She didn't care she was being cliché; he so fit the stereotype of tall, dark and handsome. 'Mm—not bad at all.'

'So you haven't answered me.' He stared at her.

'Answered what?' She feigned ignorance.

He rolled his eyes at her games. 'You know exactly what I'm talking about. What are you trying to do here?' he spoke slowly.

Her face reddened again as though she had been caught with her hand in the metaphorical cookie jar. Why she cared what this weirdo thought of her she didn't know. She tried to remain flippant. 'Well, um, you see, I'm done with this world,' she mumbled the words, hoping he wouldn't stare at her with those amazing eyes. So not fair. She wasn't immune to their hypnotic charm.

'Oh, I see.'

'"Oh, you see." What exactly do you see?' She swallowed the sting of yet another person who didn't give a shit if she simply evaporated from this world. But then again, why should this stranger give a crap when no one else in her life did? She rubbed her nose so he couldn't see the pain on her face.

'What I see is a young girl playing a dangerous game. That's what I see.' He looked out towards the horizon, where the sun cast its final glow. His jaw twitched. He looked seriously pissed at her.

Starlah stared at his profile and her heart hammered against her ribs. Maybe he did care. What was it about this man sitting next to her that caused her heart and lungs to go nuts simply by being in his presence?

He really did seem familiar to her, despite the booze effect. The way his longish hair flicked out at the sides, the way his chin pouted out slightly, but most of all, the way her body remembered his.

She shook her head: absolutely crazy. She knew she had never met him before, not in this life, as he had told her. Well then, how?

She looked away and stared at the vodka bottle. She had managed to down half its contents – a pretty good effort. She could still feel his eyes on her. They literally felt as though they burned into her. She tried to shake off the shiver playing along her spine.

'I never would have imagined you to be such a coward.' He leaned his head back on the log and stared up at the first stars kissing the night's sky.

She put her head down. 'Sorry. Suppose it was a stupid idea.' She pushed the bottle away from her and stared at the pills sitting in their piles and waiting patiently for her.

Her stomach churned in protest to the vodka sloshing around in there. Its contents burned into the lining of her stomach. For a moment she thought that her stranger was about to see what was in her stomach. She gritted her teeth and forced it to stay put.

The effects of the alcohol travelling through her bloodstream kicked in and she sunk further down the log. She was almost lying flat on the ground with her head resting against the log, the bark pulling on her light blonde hair. She was too drunk to care.

'Yeah, I'm sorry, too. I'm sorry that you felt so alone that you thought this was your only way out.' He swallowed hard and rolled onto his side so he was facing her. He propped his elbow onto the log and rested his head against his hand, his eyes scrutinising her.

Words were becoming harder to grab on to. They seemed to stick to the roof of her mouth. She tried to push the words out. 'Don't shnow why you give a shi-t.' She wiped the drool from her mouth. A part of her knew that she should be afraid of him, but she figured that if he killed her he'd be doing her and the animals a favour.

She rolled over onto her side with exaggerated effort, making loud grunting noises. She tried to imitate him and prop herself up but ended up with her head resting against her bicep.

She squinted, focusing on his features. His dreamy eyes still sparkled, even in the dark. She fixed her gaze upon his lips and for a brief moment she thought she remembered how they felt. She licked her lips and closed her eyes, taking in a deep breath.

Somewhere in the deep recesses of her mind, she heard a name being whispered—*Ardaleigh*. She opened her eyes and stared back into his. She'd swear that the space between them had become smaller.

She could feel his breath against her face. Sure, it may have been the breeze, but the breeze surely couldn't feel so sweet. She clumsily reached out and touched his lips. They felt deliciously soft and full.

He laughed and the vibration of it resonated through her body, relaxing every muscle. He raised his hand and gently swiped away a strand of her hair that was matted in her eyelashes.

The softness of his touch, the sweetness of his breath and the beauty of his face, not to mention his amazingly cut body, caused her body to heat up to feverish pitch. Or maybe it was just the vodka. Either way, she didn't protest.

She leaned into his body. She was now only a hands-breadth away. She had to fight her instincts to run her hands along his stomach. Even though his T-shirt covered his torso she just knew that he had a smooth, hair-free chest with a small tuft of soft dark hair travelling down from his navel. She gasped as she imagined tracing her finger down its path.

'Stop that,' he said, grinning.

'Stop what?' she purred.

'Stop undressing me with your eyes,' he teased.

Starlah licked her lips trying to be seductive, but in her drunken awkwardness she probably looked more like a cow chewing on a cud – sexy, indeed. She attempted to trace her finger across his lips and accidentally poked him in the eye.

'Oww …' He shut the injured eye and smiled, looking at her with his good eye. 'Seriously, Starlah, you make the worst drunk ever.' He seemed to remember something, and his smile faded. A crease formed between his brows.

She hated seeing it there. She reached up to smooth it out, but he intercepted her hand, probably too afraid he was gonna lose the other eye.

Starlah frowned when she finally registered what he said. 'Hey, how do you know my name?'

He sighed and traced his index finger along the side of her face. 'There isn't a great deal I don't know about you,' he whispered in a throaty voice.

A shiver ricocheted through her body again. Her body and mind were at odds with each other. Her head was telling her that she should flee from this hot-as weirdo, but her body was sinking further into his space. Despite her unease, she put her head against his firm shoulder.

Her body was winning the argument. Suppose if she actually lived through the night, she could blame it on the booze. 'Well, you seem to know a lot about me, and I don't even know your name.' She drooled onto his shoulder, leaving behind a patch of saliva. He didn't seem to mind.

'Mmm OK. I'll remind you then—Ardaleigh.'

'Ardaleigh,' she whispered back as her body and mind drifted off into a drunken slumber. For some weird reason she found herself slurring, 'I love you.'

'I'll always love you, my beautiful starlight, and I'll always watch over you.' He leaned in and kissed her softly on top of her silken hair, sending ripples of energy through her body.

As she dove deeper into unconsciousness, she felt him dematerialise, leaving her body shivering as the coolness of the earth's undergrowth replaced his warm body. She hugged herself and allowed the effects of the vodka to take her into a numbing darkness. The last thing she saw was his brilliant blue eyes fade to brown and a dripping tongue about to lick her face.

STARLAH ROSE fumbled with her silver clutch purse as it vibrated on her lap. She tried to answer the phone before it stopped ringing. You would think it would be an easy task, given it was just a clutch purse and not her usual suitcase of a bag. The fact it was ringing was a novelty. Her friends were all 'text-only' types of gals.

'Freaking hell,' she blurted as she dropped her phone onto the cab's floor amongst the mysterious debris and odour. She fumbled beneath the seat, trying to secure a hold around it. *Ah, come here, you stupid thing.* She finally grasped it with the aid of all the diamantes. She smiled, feeling justified for having all that bling covering her phone case.

She could hear a faint ... 'Hello—hello.'

Not wanting to bring the phone anywhere near her face, she switched it to speaker. 'Hello.'

'Ah, hel-lo, what took you so long?' Bella Todd's voice echoed around the cab's interior.

'Sorry, dropped the stupid thing.' Starlah turned her phone around, inspecting it for any foreign matter. Is that a rogue carrot piece? She flicked it off and chose to ignore it, but it could explain the suspicious odour.

'Did you break it?'

'No, I'm sitting in the back of a cab.'

'Oh. Well, tell that useless cabbie to hurry up and get your birthday butt here. Brad and I are waiting patiently for you, and you know I can only handle so much patience before I turn …' Bella's voiced became muffled as though she turned away. 'What's the opposite of patient?' Starlah could faintly hear her ask. Then Bella was back, giggling, 'Yes, that's right, impatient.'

Starlah darted her eyes towards the cabbie and shrugged in apology for Bella's insult.

He shrugged in return. 'Eh, had worse thrown at me.'

Starlah smiled at him. He resumed his focus on the usual Friday night traffic through Main Beach.

'Yeah, I know how you get when you're impatient. Gawd, look out.' Starlah giggled.

Starlah heard a guy's voice talking in the background. 'Hey, is that Brad as in your brother Brad?' She hoped not; there was something seriously off about that guy. He definitely had the creep vibe about him. He reminded her of her father. It wasn't anything tangible; she just felt uncomfortable around him. On the other hand, Bella oozed warmth and joy. From the first moment they met three years ago, she felt completely comfortable around her.

She had met Brad last year at Christmas when she tagged along to the Todd family beach house holiday. At first he seemed okay, but as the week progressed his constant accidental contact and close proximity caused a physical response in her, something along the lines of when a snake slithers across your skin. Maybe that was an overreaction, but he definitely wasn't her type so she hoped Bella wasn't trying to set the two of them up. *Eeek.*

'Yeah, Brad was eager to help celebrate your big twenty-first birthday … so hurry up, birthday girl, we can't start without you,' Bella said.

'OK chill, I'm like five minutes away. So, are you gonna tell me what my birthday surprise is?' The only info she had previously gotten out of Bella was: dress to impress, be prepared for a lot of food and alcohol, and the return of something lost. The return of something lost intrigued her. What the hell could that mean? Her stomach fluttered in anticipation.

'Oh Starlah, my bestie, as if I'm going to dish the dirt on my own surprise. Anyway stop talking, you're chewing into my credit. I'll see ya in a few.' She hung up before Starlah could say goodbye.

Starlah stared at the phone screen. Typical Bella: her wild chestnut red hair and lustrous green eyes matched her wild personality. And she was sure that Bella had something wild set up for tonight. Being unaccustomed to Bella's level of wild, Starlah had to admit she was nervous as to how the night would evolve. Last time they all went out, Bella almost got arrested for pinching a cute police officer's butt. Starlah still cringed every time she passed a cute cop, looking over her shoulder to make sure that Bella wasn't anywhere nearby.

The cab slammed on its brakes and Starlah went flying forward, almost connecting with the front seat's head rest. Thankfully, she had remembered to put the seat belt on before they left. *Now wouldn't that have been a party pleaser?* Blood dripping down her sapphire-blue baby doll dress.

'Get the hell outta my way, you bloody morons,' the cabbie yelled out the window. He seemed to remember he had a passenger and flicked his eyes to the rear-view mirror. 'Sorry, you OK?' He shook his head. 'Those bloody tourists drive me crazy with those mopeds. If they don't know how to bloody ride that pathetic excuse for a vehicle, then they shouldn't be on the road. Hey?' He stared at her, waiting for her to confirm.

'Yeah, I know right? What's the go with them hogging the road like that?' Starlah stared out the window, giving them her best pissed-off glare. Too bad the windows were tinted.

The cabbie slammed his hand onto the horn. 'Move!' The assembly gradually dispersed, allowing them to pass. 'Bloody morons,' the cabbie affirmed as he sped away.

Starlah smiled. She liked him. She wished she were more vocal at times.

'You a local girl then?' He looked back up into the rear-view mirror.

'Yep, born and bred on the Gold Coast.' She nodded.

'Yeah, me too. Nothing like it hey?' He nodded proudly.

Starlah wasn't so sure she felt the same. There wasn't anything about her upbringing on the Gold Coast that she felt proud about. All she had to do was picture the dilapidated state of the front yard of her parents' house, with the unruly hedges, mammoth mound of cigarette butts and beer cans, and deep shame trumped any moments of pride. She couldn't believe she had allowed Jasmine Harrison, her co-worker back at the DVD store she used to work at, to help her pack and get away from her parent's abusive control.

Thankfully, Jaz had seemed immune to the filth, or maybe she had been trying her best to show Starlah courage and support. Either way, Starlah was eternally grateful. Jaz was the only person back then who showed any real care factor about her, except maybe Bella. She pictured Jaz's kind, blue eyes and hoped Bella had invited her to her birthday 'thing', whatever that was.

Finally they navigated through the chaos on Sea World Drive and arrived in front of the main strip in Mariner's Cove. The cabbie pulled over to the side and shoved the gear into neutral.

'Here you go, love. That's forty-five bucks, thanks.' He turned his body so he could look at her.

She fished through her purse and pulled out a fifty. 'Thanks, keep the change.' She smiled at him. She had enjoyed his banter.

'Oh thanks, love, you have yourself a great night. Oh, and happy birthday.' He grinned, showing deep laugh lines around his eyes.

Starlah self-consciously felt around her own eyes, wondering if any had sprung up over the day, hoping it wasn't time for Botox just yet. Now that she was twenty-one it was a possibility. She figured if it did happen, it would be a good thing anyway, right?

Meant she had laughed a lot in her life, though that wouldn't actually be true. She shrugged to herself and the cabbie, knowing that the crows hadn't had a chance to land any feet on her face yet.

Starlah opened the cab door and swung her legs out, jumping up eagerly. She turned to close the door and her airy sapphire-blue dress decided to make an announcement of her arrival by flying up over her head. It billowed up and flashed her lacy boy-cut undies to innocent bystanders. It didn't care that it was still a PG time slot and kids were walking past. Thankfully, she hadn't gone with the G-string variety.

She grimaced, still gripping the handle and debating whether to jump straight back into the car, but the cabbie's chuckles halted her. 'Hey, I just gave you a five-dollar tip.' She frowned at him.

'Arh don't worry about that, sweetheart, got nuffin' to be ashamed of there.' He grinned even wider. 'But I hope you put some antiseptic on that carpet burn.' He stared down at her knees.

Carpet burn? What? She darted her eyes down to her knees. *Oh God.* 'No. Not carpet burn … treadmill incident.' She stared at him, her mouth gaping. *Seriously, what the hell?*

She looked back down at her knees and caught a glimpse of something reflecting off her legs. She scrunched her eyes and everything became magnified. *Oh crap.* She shook her head. She had forgotten the note to self about the de-fuzzing duties she was supposed to undertake *before* leaving the house. No wonder when she was walking to the cab her dress was getting caught on something: stubble. It was amazing it didn't cause a static flame. Bella often remarked on her peaches and cream complexion. Maybe that's what she meant by peaches: fuzzy.

Just perfect.

She gave the cabbie one final glare as she slammed the door. She straightened her dress and smoothed her golden tresses and took in a deep breath. *OK, no one else saw that. Good. And hopefully, no one will notice the other condition.*

'Woo hoo, sex kitten alert,' Starlah heard from behind her. She turned to see Bella and her brother walking towards her.

Oh, great. Absolutely freaking fantastic.

Bella clapped her hands. 'You sure do know how to make an entrance, birthday girl.' She sashayed towards her, standing out in her golden sequinned mini and sheer black boobtube. She wasn't even struggling to walk in her high, golden, glittery Jimmy Choos.

'No—I can't believe you saw that.' Starlah turned her back to her friend and covered her face, feeling the heat radiating off her cheeks. The fact Brad was leering at her wasn't helping much.

'Ah come here, silly. No biggie. We've all flashed in public before.' Bella grabbed her, spun her around and smacked her lips onto her burning cheeks. 'Happy birthday.' She pushed her out. 'Now let me have a good look at you.'

Starlah held her breath; *Here we go.* Unlike Bella, who loved devouring and judging all the fashion mags, Starlah's knowledge of fashion and brand names was very limited, and it showed in her usual casual jeans and T-shirt daily uniform. But she did try super hard to look the part for tonight.

She had spent hours contemplating what she should wear. It had been a battle between the satin black number that hugged her body, showing off her toned thighs, or the silk baby doll one. In the end, it was the way the blue silk dress flowed in soft waves, making her feel feminine, that won her over.

The trade-off for losing two dress sizes was that there wasn't much left of her chest, and she had to rely on other ways to show off her feminine charm. Growing up with her parents' heavy-handed approach to parenting, she became acquainted with the notion of comfort eating. It had taken her two years to break that habit when she left, but now she couldn't ever imagine returning there. Well, she hoped not, anyway.

'Not bad, not bad at all.' Bella nodded. 'I see you took my advice and highlighted those amazing brown eyes of yours with soft earth tones.' She peered in close and studied Starlah's eyes. 'See, I told you that colour would bring out the cinnamon flecks. Beautiful. Absolutely.' She planted another hard kiss against her cheek, leaving behind a bright red lipstick stamp.

Brad pushed Bella out of the way. 'My turn.' He seized Starlah around both arms and leaned in to kiss her on the cheek.

Her skin crawled. She closed her eyes and hoped he would be quick.

He lingered and audibly inhaled, almost sucking up her hair into his nostrils. 'Mm, love that vanilla, and thanks for the show.' He grinned at her.

She pulled back, involuntarily scrunching up her nose. She couldn't say the same about his overpowering scent. Hadn't he heard of the saying, a little goes a long way? *Obviously not.*

And as to the show – *No, not a show.* Seriously, what the hell was going on?

'OK, you two, enough of that. We better go inside.' Bella looped her arm through Starlah's and dragged her towards Versace's.

'Oh, my God, are we going in there for dinner?' Starlah's eyes lit up. She had never been anywhere this fancy before.

'Close, we're going to de Brie's Cavern.' Bella's face beamed. 'I know how much you fancy checking out his sexy biceps, watching that cooking show.'

'Are you serious? You got a table at his restaurant? Wow, you must have booked it weeks ago.' Starlah squeezed Bella's arm. 'Ooh, so excited. I hope he's on tonight and I get a sneak peek at those sexy black curls and green eyes.'

Bella laughed, 'Not to mention his cute butt, hey?'

Brad frowned; he didn't seem to be amused.

Starlah didn't care. It was her birthday. 'You bet,' she giggled.

STARLAH COULD barely keep it together, walking through the foyer of the restaurant. All she wanted to do was squeal and clap her hands, revealing her socially inept traits to the whole world, but she didn't want to commit complete social suicide and kept herself in control. But hey, it was hard work, given the foyer did look like a gateway to heaven. Well, maybe Starlah's food fantasy version of heaven, anyway. She expected to hear a faint angelic *aaahhh* in the background. That's how amazing the place looked.

The lighting was soft, warm and complimenting, and the mirrors seemed to reflect the best version of you. Which is what you wanted, really, the lighting to lie a little, so you walk in feeling good about yourself, eat and drink a heap and not care what you looked like on the way out. Maybe there was a back, non-mirrored exit.

At the end of the magical mirror corridor, beneath a massive picture of Mr Sexy Chef, was a pompous, upturned-nosed gentleman. OK, maybe that's how he was born, but his demeanour suited the place, giving the illusion they were being treated by royalty.

'Good evening, how may I help you?' He stood to attention in his black suit-white shirt combo. He didn't smile.

'Look out, looks like he's about to land a kiss with those pursed suckers,' Bella whispered behind her hand.

Starlah tried not to giggle as she stared at lips that looked as though he was sucking on a sour bomb.

'Yes, good evening, we have a table for six, booked under Starlah Rose. Thank you.' Bella tried to match his pompousness, but came off mockingly.

He barely moved his head and scanned down the page. 'Ah, yes indeed.' He raised his hand, and a young guy about eighteen came running and stood to attention.

'Please seat these guests at number twenty-nine.' He nodded slightly, cast his eyes down and was done with them.

Arh, OK … thanks.

'Ooh, this is so exciting, Bells. I can't believe you kept this from me for so long. Not like you at all; usually your loose lips get in the way.' Starlah clutched her by the arm as they followed the young, jittery waiter. She wondered if he was related to the 'sour bomb' guy.

The waiter manoeuvred his way around the tables until he came to the back of the room near the toilets. 'Here you go …' He waved around the table, bouncing from one foot to the other, as though the only reason he put them near the toilet was so he could dart in there himself.

Starlah couldn't stop staring at his oversized white shirt that he must have borrowed from the front desk guy. She tried in vain not to look down to his black slacks, which were hitched a fraction too high and showing off far too much info. She darted her eyes back up into his face and smiled warmly at him.

Thinking it was best to stop staring at the poor guy, she walked over to a chair and pulled it out. He responded, grabbed the back of the chair and pushed it in as she sat, and then he did the same for Bella. He didn't bother with Brad's, as he'd already seated himself. Besides, who'd want to go near that scowling face anyway?

'Wow, this is amazing. Thanks so much for this.' Starlah redirected her focus to the breathtaking view around the restaurant. The restaurant's back wall was one continuous window overlooking the Broadwater. The twinkling lights off the yachts and distant buildings looked magical. There was a light classical violin number playing softly in the background. The lighting remained soft and warm.

Starlah breathed in the aroma from the kitchen. She found herself licking her lips in anticipation. Brad caught her lick and stared at her mouth, his scowl turning into a flirty smirk. She looked away. She didn't want to encourage his attention.

The tables were set up to offer guests some privacy. No doubt, with having celebrities visiting, they had to come up with a design that offered as much seclusion as possible in a public environment. Secluded booths lined the windows and side walls. Except for their table, they seemed to be in the middle of a walkway.

'I can't believe they shoved us in the back, next to that.' Bella pointed towards the men's bathroom. She pouted her lips as she did whenever she didn't get her way. Clearly, she didn't feel the need to be so close to the lavatory quarters.

'Bells, it's wonderful. Really, it is.' Starlah beamed, feeling drunk on the atmosphere. She wasn't going to complain, given how she spent her previous birthdays … mm, let's see, Macca's by herself, hiding from her parents pretty much most birthdays, and there was that one time at Hog's Breath when the neighbour's kid took her out on a date for her sixteenth birthday and he tried getting a little too much reward for his money.

Starlah looked at Bella and had to smile. It wasn't her fault she was accustomed to more decadence and had perceived their seating as an insult.

'Yeah, but I expected better treatment than this,' Bella sulked.

'Bells, it's all good. Really, you did a great job.' Brad smiled at her.

Starlah stared at him and wondered if she had him wrong. He was always so attentive and supportive of Bella. Her a-hole radar must be on the blink.

'Fine, suppose it will do.' Bella continued to pout as she surveyed the room, and then her face lit up. 'Hey, Jaz, is here,' she announced.

Starlah spun her head around and smiled as Jasmine made her way to the table, looking dazzling in her blood-red satin and ruched bodice dress, complementing her short, cropped, platinum-blonde hair. A good-looking guy was following close by; it must be her new boyfriend, Nate.

'OMG. He is so lava-lish,' Bella blurted as she leapt up and raced towards them. She threw her arms around Jasmine's neck and eyed off her man. 'Now who do we have here?' she purred as she let go of Jasmine's neck and stuck out her hand to greet him.

'Hi, Bella. This is Nate.' Jasmine smiled nervously.

Nate wrapped his arm around Jasmine and nodded. 'Hey.' He grinned, revealing perfect white teeth, standing out in contrast to his tanned, handsome face. He finally seemed to notice Bella's hand, and he leaned in and shook her hand.

Bella flipped her hair and flashed her equally white teeth. 'Welcome, Nate, so nice to meet you.' She grinned as she looped her arm through Jasmine's and led them to the table.

'Jaz, you sly minx, where have you been hiding him?' She continued to linger her eyes over Nate's muscular form.

Starlah knew exactly why Jasmine hadn't introduced Nate to Bella before. This was a perfect example *why*. 'Hi, Nate. I'm Starlah.' She got to her feet and shook his hand.

'Hey, happy birthday.' He smiled as he shook her hand.

Brad just sat there and glared at Nate, asserting his alpha status. Poor bastard looked totally ordinary in his dark-blue T-shirt, which hung loosely over his lean, non-bulging arms. Brad was definitely what you would call Mr Average: average height, average build, light-brown hair and sharp, icy blue eyes. He wrapped his arms around himself in a defensive pose.

Yeah, good onya. Starlah looked over at him and frowned. That was why she was confused about her a-hole radar.

'Please, have a seat,' Starlah offered, extending her hand.

'Yes, have a seat.' Bella came around the back of both of them and placed her arms across their shoulders. They both pulled out a chair and sat down.

'Hey,' Nate greeted Brad.

'Hi,' Brad responded with a false smile.

Starlah reluctantly sat herself next to Brad and looked at the sixth chair. 'So who's the mystery guest?' She pointed to the empty chair.

Bella shrugged. 'You'll just have to wait and see, birthday girl.'

Starlah caught a glimpse out the corner of her eye of a figure approaching their table. At first, her conscious brain didn't recognise him, but her heart knew. It galloped erratically. All her attention honed in on the figure. There was something familiar about that walk and the way he smiled at her.

Her brain shuffled through her memory pit and spat out the only conclusion that made sense: Daniel. Could it really be? It had been ten years since he had run away from their parents' home; he had been fifteen and she had been eleven. He never looked back, and now somehow …

'Oh, my God, are you serious?' Starlah put her hand over her mouth, and her eyes misted over. It really *was* Daniel.

He approached, grinning, holding out a small box, gift-wrapped beautifully. He stood beside her chair and hesitated. 'Happy birthday, Starbright,' he said, planting a warm kiss on her red cheek.

She shook her head and then jumped up and threw her arms around his neck. 'Oh, my God. I can't believe you're actually here—but how—who?' She held her brother tight. She looked over to Bella, who was beaming, clasping her hands. She noted Bella's eyes were teary.

'Do you like your birthday surprise?' Bella clapped her hands. 'Told you I was going to return something lost.'

Starlah reluctantly let go of her brother, went over to Bella and gave her a big hug. 'Thank you so much.' She let a tear wash down her cheek. 'I thought I would never see him again, thank you.' She didn't know how Bella had managed to find him, when she had failed to do so over the years.

'No probs, Starbright,' Bella said.

Starlah hadn't been called that since she last saw Daniel. That painful day was still etched through her memory and had replayed itself often over the years: he sat on the edge of her bed, holding a pink stuffed teddy as he woke her. He was dressed in a black hoodie, which covered his shaggy blond hair. She remembered her heart pounding as he said his good-byes.

'Starbright, you know that I love ya, right?' He fumbled for the right words. He didn't wait for her to answer. 'But I just can't stick around this hellhole and put up with Dad and his . . .' He stared out the window.

'Danny, what's happening?' Her innocent, eleven-year-old brain tried desperately to understand what he was trying to say.

'You gotta listen. I'm leaving, and I ain't coming back.' He refused to look into her eyes.

'No, Danny, you can't leave me here by myself, please.' She sat up, rubbing her eyes.

'Starlah, if I don't leave … if he doesn't kill me, then I'm afraid I might kill him.' His voice was strained.

Starlah cried and wrapped her skinny arms around his waist.

He squeezed her tight for a moment, and then pulled her arms off him. 'I gotta go.' He handed her the teddy and stood in the middle of the room, the moon casting eerie shadows across his face. He looked tormented. 'Remember … Starlight, star bright, the first star I see … I'll think of you, Starlah.' And with that, he left her room and life for the next ten years.

Starlah shook her head again. She just couldn't believe he was actually here.

The waiter interrupted. 'Is everyone ready for some champagne?' He held up a bottle that Bella must have pre-ordered.

'Oh yeah, sure.' Starlah darted her eyes around, suddenly aware that everyone had been staring at her. She went back over to her seat and sat down. She looked at Brad. 'Do you mind if Daniel sits here?' He begrudgingly moved over a seat, and she patted the seat next to her. 'Sit here, Daniel.'

He took his seat next to her. He darted his eyes around the table self-consciously. 'Um, hi, everyone. I'm Daniel, Starlah's brother.'

They all returned their greetings in unison, and after the waiter finished pouring them all a glass, Daniel raised his. He cleared his throat, saying, 'Here's to Starlah, happy birthday, Sis. I know I've missed a lot of your birthdays in the past, but I hope to be around for the next twenty-one.' He sipped the liquid and smiled.

She lifted her glass and took a sip. She didn't mind the bubbly kiss it offered her. Her heart beamed with joy and pride as she sat next to her big brother. She ignored the swirling of unanswered questions pounding on the door, wanting to burst out and ruin the party.

She looked him over. He had grown so much, from a scrawny teen to this handsome man. She studied his features. His caramel eyes still held the cheeky spark that their dad had never been able to knock out of him. His hair was short, but still held that sun-kissed look. He'd grown so tall. She came to just below his shoulders. She was five-foot eight; he had to be six-foot three. She noticed the tattoos on one of his biceps, but couldn't see what they were.

She looked back up and studied his face. There was something different about him. He looked as though he was haunted. It was in the way he kept looking over at her, like he felt guilty, or maybe she was seeing what she thought ought to be there.

He remembered the gift he still clutched in his other hand. 'Here you go. Hope you like it. I wasn't really sure what you would be into these days. Sorry.' He looked down at the table.

She reached for the gift and smiled, deciding to focus on the magic of this moment, not on all the unanswered questions. 'Thanks heaps, Danny.' She wrapped her hand around his. 'Seriously, thank you.' She stared into his eyes.

He lifted his eyes up and grinned cheekily, and she almost lost it. He looked like the Danny from all those years ago, and the pain reservoir cracked and demanded attention, tugging at her heart and tear ducts. She had to look away and feign coughing and sneezing, anything to halt the reservoir's deterioration.

When she felt more in control, she stared down at the red box, tied up with a golden ribbon. It looked beautifully done, as though a lot of love and attention went into preparing it. She swallowed the insolent, demanding hurt and allowed herself to feel excited.

She untied the ribbon and peeled back the wrapping paper. Inside was a red, velvety jewellery box. She opened the box and gasped. 'Oh, Danny. It's beautiful.' She touched the pendant inside.

Bella leaned over. 'Show me, show me.' She stuck her head just about into Starlah's lap. 'Wow, it's beautiful.'

'Where did you find it?' Starlah pulled it out of the box and examined it closely. She turned it around, catching the light reflecting off the varied colours. She'd never seen anything like it.

'Just in this funky gift shop. It's a Melody's Stone. If you look closely, you can see seven different crystals blended together into a flame.' He shrugged. 'Don't know, just thought of you when I came across it.'

'So you remember all my crazy crystal play?' Starlah continued to examine the pendant.

He nodded. 'Yeah, I remember Crystal Princess casting magic spells with her stones. What was it that you used to call them?' He smiled at her.

'My wishing stones.' She turned red. 'OK, OK, so I used to live in a fantasy world—I know.' She remembered that the fantasy world offered her a reprieve from the madness of her real world and saved her many times from truly going insane.

She stared at the pendant again. She had never seen anything like it. It was such a beautiful and thoughtful gift from her brother.

'Do you want me to put it on for you?' Jasmine asked, saving her from blabbering all over them.

Starlah handed the pendant over to Jasmine, turned and lifted up her straight, shoulder-length hair, so she could clasp the chain around her neck. When it was securely fastened to her neck, she turned back around and ran her fingers over the pendant. It felt warm, and her fingers tingled. It was as though the thing vibrated against her skin. Mm, weird, she thought, but it also felt comforting and familiar, like it had always belonged to her.

'Suits you.' Jasmine smiled.

Starlah looked into Daniel's eyes. 'Thank you. It really is perfect.'

He nodded and took another sip of the champagne. He still looked uncomfortable.

The waiter came back over and asked if everyone was ready to order.

'Is Chef Marcus de Brie cooking tonight?' Bella asked.

The waiter cleared his throat. 'Yes, ma'am.' He held his pen poised, ready to write down their orders. It appeared he still hadn't gone to the toilet and he continued to bounce.

'Ma'am? Now isn't that just adorable.' Bella looked him up and down, as though being called 'ma'am' was the worst insult. She was weird about being the oldest in their group. She was twenty-two and a half.

Bella held her glare on the poor waiter until his bouncing just about propelled him to the ceiling. She finally appeared satisfied and redirected her attention back to the group. 'Oh my God, Starlah, you are absolutely going to die when you taste his food. I'm so pleased he's here for your birthday.' She darted her eyes back at the waiter, 'Right then, tell Chef de Brie we have a special birthday girl here and we want to be surprised by whatever he sees fit to cook for us.' She held up a credit card. 'Daddy won't mind paying.' She smiled at last.

Starlah smiled back. Typical. Daddy's little princess could pretty much get away with anything. She darted her eyes around the table as she caressed the pendant, feeling joy spread through her body. She had a group of amazing friends, and now she had her brother back. Life couldn't get any sweeter. She studied Daniel again. She desperately wanted to know where he had been the past ten years, but interrogating him would be a major party disruptor. The first opportunity and she hoped there would be one; she planned on asking him.

THREE

STARLAH SAT there with a massive gratified grin plastered across her face. She dropped her fork and held back a burp, given this wasn't the type of place one should engage in such debaucheries. Master Chef de Brie so did not disappoint. The celebrity ego he must have hadn't taken away any of his amazing cooking skills.

She licked her lips, savouring the lingering taste of the triple chocolate fudge cake. The white chocolate mousse complemented the decadently rich and moist layers of chocolate cake and frosting. She patted her stomach in complete satisfaction. 'Mm, a-ma-zing. Thanks Bella, you are a legend. Oh and thanks, sexy bum Chef,' she giggled, feeling giddy on the champagne and chocolate indulgence.

'You're most welcome, birthday girl. I'm glad you got to experience his handiwork. Now when you fantasise about him, you can imagine him spreading that chocolate mousse all over you,' Bella laughed heartily.

'Eww, not something I want to imagine my kid sister doing, thanks.' Daniel put his fingers in his ears like a schoolkid, pretending to be singing, 'La-la-la-la.'

Starlah shrugged innocently. 'Oops sorry, big bro.'

He laughed, leaned over and stuck his arm around her. 'I'll forgive you this once.' He kissed her on the side of her head.

She beamed. It still felt surreal having him do that. He had done that a million times in her dreams, but now that he was here for real, his hugs in person were a trillion times more comforting than her dreams. She completely surrendered to the joy of the experience.

Starlah caught a glimpse of Brad's scowling expression and cringed. The intensity of his glaring was seriously disrupting her party joy. *What the hell was his problem?* It eventually registered that she was staring back at him and his face changed. He smiled a wide grin as though he were enjoying the joke. *Creep.*

'OK, so I know it's relatively early, but what do you all say to going and checking out Benji's? I hear an indie cover band is starting in thirty minutes, and they're supposed to be pretty good.' Bella fluttered her long, fake lashes at everyone.

Jaz looked at Nate, Nate looked at Daniel and Daniel shrugged at Starlah.

'Yeah sure, sounds great,' Brad chirped up. After a few seconds, everyone nodded. The decision had been made.

'Absolutely fantastic. Now let's go party!' Bella led the way.

Not surprisingly, Benji's was pretty impressive. Aqua lounges decorated the back walls, and fuchsia barstools with silver round bar tables were peppered throughout. The band's stage was set up with the usual equipment: drums, guitar, keyboard, microphones and amps. The band was still setting up, so the DJ was playing random music to keep the crowd going until the band could take over.

Brad leaned in and yelled into Starlah's ear, 'I'll go get us some drinks.'

She nodded. 'OK thanks.' Anything to get him away from her. Judging by the crowd at the bar, it should take him a while.

Bella jumped up and down, clapping her hands. 'Oh I love this song. Come and dance with me.' She grabbed Jasmine's and her hands, pulling them towards the dance floor.

'No, you two go.' Starlah pulled her hand free. 'I want to catch up with my brother.' She looked over to Daniel, who was standing in the back awkwardly sipping on his drink.

Starlah walked over to him and smiled. 'You're not feeling it, are you?'

'What?' He leaned in and yelled.

'This scene. It's not really your thing, hey?'

He laughed. 'No, you're right.' He took another swig from his drink. 'I feel too old for this crowd.' He nodded towards the predominately eighteen-to-twenty-one horde, bouncing around on the dance floor.

Starlah giggled. 'I'm so happy you came. I've thought about you all the time.' A sad look crossed her face. 'Danny, I really have missed you. After you left—well, you know …'

She looked out towards Bella and Jasmine, dancing to one of her favourite songs from a few years ago: Fun's 'Some Nights'.

Bella was swinging her arms up in the air, bouncing around to the beat. Her bounteous chest, barely contained in her boobtube, was drawing attention from both genders in the crowd.

Daniel swallowed hard and stared into his drink. 'Starbright, I'm so sorry, but I didn't know what else to do.' He shook his head. 'I guess I hoped I was the one he hated and he would calm down when I left. If I had known'—he stared into her eyes—'I would have come for you.' He looked away, and a tormented grimace played across his features – the same look she remembered on the night he left.

Starlah opened her mouth. Her heart screamed, *Tell him how much it hurt being left behind,* but his haunted eyes halted her. She didn't want to risk losing him again by pushing him too far into guilt zone. She swallowed, suffocating any further whimpers.

'Ah, that's water under the bridge now. It's my birthday, and it's party time.' She inhaled and lifted her head high. Besides, it wasn't like he was the one that beat up on her. She caressed the pendant he gave her. Tears stung her eyes as the hurt reservoir churned below the surface.

'Here you go, birthday girl.' Brad handed over a massive cocktail glass.

Starlah cringed as she took the glass. 'Um, thanks.' She had no idea how the hell she was going to be able to swallow it. The massive fishbowl sloshed with multi-coloured layers of liquor. She eyed him with a suspicious glance.

Daniel stared at Brad and frowned. He leaned into Starlah and whispered into her ear. 'Be careful of that one. I don't trust him.'

She nodded. 'Thanks for caring.' She leaned into Daniel's

body, and he hugged her close. She felt like the eleven-year-old girl being comforted by her big brother from many years ago. It felt like home.

Bella looked over at them and then raced over. 'OK, enough bonding time. Come and dance with me.' She grabbed their drinks and put them on the table, then grabbed Daniel's and her hands and dragged them towards the dance floor.

'Save me,' Daniel mouthed while being spun across the dance floor.

Starlah rolled her head back, laughed and then mouthed, 'Sorry, you're on your own,' as she turned her palms up. 'Can't help you.' She giggled as she watched Bella try to get him to move his body to the beat.

He broke out into a smile and allowed himself to be led by Bella. He tried to imitate her moves: no chance. He looked more like a geek having a fit than someone trying to dance.

Starlah put her hand over her mouth and continued to giggle. How could she not totally love him in this moment? She knew his natural instinct would be to retreat. But he persevered, and her heart swelled with joy. She loved seeing him like that and secretly hoped it would be one of many times. She had missed him like crazy.

He had his hands out to the side and he unsuccessfully tried to sway his hips to the beat while tapping his left foot. So adorable. OK, it would've been more adorable if he was actually in sync with the music, but nonetheless he did look cute in his Levi's and light peach V-neck T-shirt, bopping along. He looked into Starlah's eyes and shrugged.

She winked. 'Hot stuff Danny. Big hit with the chicks.'

He stuck his thumb up. 'Yeah I know, right?' He grinned.

Brad shimmied over. Seriously, he had the shimmy thing going. He tried desperately to get in on the fun by getting up close and personal. He tried the old 'bump into her body and then pretend not to notice' trick while dancing around.

OK, so he was technically a better dancer than Daniel despite the shimmy thing, but if he touched her one more time, she was gonna kick him in the … well, let's just say he wouldn't be thinking with it for a while.

After several hours of dancing, racing off and drinking and then back to dancing and one too many 'oops sorry' from Brad, Starlah had had enough. She gritted her teeth and retreated to the sofa. Bella had the stamina of a marathon runner.

Starlah looked at Bella, and Bella raised her eyebrow and put her hands up as if to say, 'What?' Starlah fanned herself and stuck her tongue out as an explanation for her abandonment.

Bella nodded and mouthed, 'OK' and continued to dance. Daniel looked over at Starlah and then extracted his sweaty self from Bella's clutches. She pouted, flipped her hair and shrugged *whatever* before returning to her sexy moves.

Phew, Starlah thought. She knew Bella's man-hungry signals and was relieved that Daniel wasn't about to become her next victim. It wouldn't have been too long before her pouty lips gravitated towards his. Starlah's stomach contents wouldn't have coped with that.

Daniel joined her, and they both sat there exhausted, surveying the crowd. Starlah stared at Brad and his 'come hither' look to her and frowned, while Danny stared at Bella and looked relieved to be away from her.

After a while he leaned in. 'I'm gonna split. OK?'

Her heart raced as his words echoed those on the last night she saw him. She felt herself revert back to that eleven-year-old and was about to throw her arms around his waist and plead for him to not leave her again.

'No, not like that—sorry.' He grabbed her hand. 'I meant just for the night. Promise I won't leave you like that again.' He looked down. 'I'm sorry for leaving you, and I want to make it up to you, if you'll let me, Starbright.'

Her heart rate slowed and she managed to smile. 'Oh, that's OK then.' She squeezed his hand. 'I was having a flashback.' She cringed.

'Yeah, I noticed.' He leaned over and kissed her on the side of her head. 'Are we all good?'

'Yeah, we're good. You have no idea how happy I am to have you back. This time I won't let you disappear. I'll hunt you down if you do.' She pointed at him, giving him her best fake-stern look before breaking out into a smile. She reached over and hugged him hard.

He hugged her back just as hard then pulled away. 'Give me your phone.' He sat up and stuck out his hand.

She looked at him and then realised what he was doing. She handed over her phone.

He entered his number into her contacts. 'Here, now you can track me down easily.' He smiled and got up. 'Give me a call when you want to catch up. Love ya, Starbright. See ya soon.' He turned and made his way through the jumping crowd.

Starlah watched him dodge the crowd as he made his way to the door. He stopped there and waved. She waved back and smiled, confident she would see him again.

She continued to stare at the door, and a small walled-off corner of her brain peeled back to relive sweet memories of Daniel. Unfortunately, with the memories of Daniel came flooding back the memories of her parents, and the reservoir's wall cracked wide open and spewed out a haunting memory.

'Starlah you stupid bitch, where the fuck are my pills?' Her mother rummaged through her dresser. 'I know you've done something with them.'

Starlah could hear her mum going off in the next room. She recoiled and hugged her pillow. She knew what was coming.

'First you fuck off for the whole night, and now I can't find my pills. I swear, if you took them I'm gonna kill ya.' The echo of items being tossed and smashed vibrated through the wall and into her heart.

The hangover gripped her brain so tight, she thought it would ooze out of her ears. She hadn't factored failing into her equation, and now being alive and back home, she would pay for taking their pills and booze. She readied herself.

Her mother burst through the door and stood there heaving. Her dirty blonde hair fizzed out in a halo around her head. Her dull, bloodshot russet-coloured eyes glared venomously at her. 'So Miss High Almighty, where are they?'

If looks could kill, she would surely be free by now – if only. 'I don't know, Mum ...' she pleaded, cowering further back so she was now pressed up against the head of the bed. The pillow protested her fierce grip, squeaking. She'd swear the walls cringed in sympathy with her. They too were saturated with years of yelling and smashed objects and trickles of blood.

Her mum edged her way towards Starlah and stopped right at the foot of her bed. She darted her eyes erratically around the room, trying to detect her deceit. 'Really, so how come on the same day you fuck off God knows where, is the same day they go missing?' She seemed to be sniffing the room like a hound on a blood trail.

Starlah's heart pounded. Her hands trembled. Her ribs contracted, waiting for the onslaught. She closed her eyes and tried to picture the stranger's soothing eyes. Ardaleigh.

SLAP. A sting across her face snapped them open. 'Don't fuckin' close your eyes when I'm talking to you. Where are they?' she yelled into Starlah's face, leaning over the bed with her hands on her wide doughy hips.

Starlah snapped. 'Yeah I fucking took them. So what? And they were great.' Tears poured down her red-hot face as she wished that were true.

'You—you—' Her mother pointed at her in rage.

She heard her father yelling in the kitchen. Obviously, he just discovered his vodka was missing. She could hear him storming towards her room, rambling about what he was going to do to her. He stumbled through the door and stood there huffing, red-faced. It took him a few moments to comprehend what he was seeing, and then he frowned, probably pissed that her mum got to her first.

'Do you know what this piece of shit did?' Her mum fumed. 'Stole my fucking pills, she did.'

Her dad stumbled towards them, still wearing the effects of last night's binge. 'So Little Miss thought she'd throw herself a party, did she?' He scratched the side of his scruffy face while glaring at Starlah.

'What she take of yours?' Her mum continued to hold her hands on her hips, but a smirk played across her lips.

He walked towards them, undoing his belt. 'Did you enjoy my vodka?' He tilted his head, 'Did you find what you were looking for in it?' He pulled the belt out and let it dangle in front of Starlah.

Her mother nodded. 'Yeah. Did ya?' Her face lit up.

Starlah crawled up into the corner of her bed, turned over and put the pillow over her head, hoping it would protect her already throbbing skull. Her back and ribs were exposed to her parents. She gritted her teeth and braced herself for their tag-team assault.

'Shit, Starlah, are you OK?'

Starlah stared vacantly ahead.

'You look all pale and sweaty.' Jasmine sat down beside her.

Starlah shook her head and then darted her eyes around, clutching her ribs and holding her breath. 'What?'

'What's the matter?' Jasmine placed her arm around her.

Starlah swallowed hard and looked down at her clenched hands. 'Nothing. I'm fine, just overdid it on the cocktails …' She looked over at Bella's glass to see how much of her own drink was left in it. Bella never noticed that her glass seemed to remain the same with every mouthful.

Starlah rubbed her throat as the room spun around her. Her senses were overloaded by the bombarding noise. She jumped up. 'I'll be back in a minute.' She needed to get away. She heard Jasmine asking if she wanted her to come with her.

Starlah shook her head, raced to the bathroom, locked herself in a cubicle and heaved, shallow painful breaths. She rummaged through her purse to see if there was anything in there to help her slow her breathing down. In the end she used the purse to breathe into, focusing on slow, deep breaths.

There was a tap at the toilet door. 'Starlah, are you OK?' Bella's voice seeped through the door.

Starlah flicked her hands a few times and took a slow steady breath in. 'Yeah, all good now.' She opened the door and exhaled, wiping her hand across her mouth, pretending to be wiping vomit off her face. Bella loved it when Starlah partied as hard as she did.

'Oh honey, I think you've had enough, hey.' She grabbed Starlah by the shoulders and led her to the sink. 'Come on, clean yourself up. I'll get Brad to drive you home.' Bella smiled.

Starlah's heart palpitated a few times. 'No, I'm fine. I'll just catch a cab.' She looked into the mirror at her red-rimmed eyes and grimaced. She really did look like she was well over the limit.

'Rubbish. I ain't letting no BFF of mine to ride alone in some weirdo's cab at three-thirty in the morning. No way. Brad would be more than happy to drive you.' She ushered her out of the bathroom back through the moshing crowd and straight into Brad's eager arms.

Oh, shit …

FOUR

S O YOU GONNA invite me in?' Brad stood at the threshold to her two-bedroom duplex and stared into the lounge room, waiting for her to step back and let him in.

Starlah sighed. She was tired and overwhelmed and just wanted to go to bed.

She felt a whisper brush the back of her neck. *Don't let him in.* It traced along her spine.

She took a few of steps in and turned around to say goodnight. He was standing right behind her. He'd invited himself in.

'Nice place.' He surveyed her living area, nodding at her décor. He seemed to like her dark chocolate faux suede L-shaped lounge, framing the corner of her small living area. It faced her forty inch plasma TV.

He walked over and fingered through her DVD collection. 'Got some pretty cool DVDs. Maybe we could watch one.' He turned and grinned at her. 'Bella gave me instructions to wait until I thought you were OK.' He turned back around and picked up a DVD.

Starlah stood at the door, frozen. He wasn't going to be easy to get rid of. Why the hell did she let Bella talk her into letting him drive her home? No doubt he was well over the limit, and he was definitely well over her limit of being able to tolerate him.

He laughed at her. 'Come over here, silly, and close the door. Don't want the neighbours complaining about the noise.'

Fine, she thought, she would indulge him for a few moments and then he would be satisfied and leave. She reluctantly shuffled over, stood at the foot of the lounge and stared at the DVD in his hand. *Great,* he would have to pick that one up. It was one of a rare few psycho-thrillers she had. She winced. Was he telling her something?

Get rid of him now, came the whisper, only louder and definitely male in origin. A shudder worked its way through her back and into her arms. What the hell was that?

'Oh, I love this movie—love how he manages to trick his victims into trusting him and then has his way with them.' He turned the DVD over so he could read the back of it. A smirk played across his lips.

She felt a twist in her stomach. She tried to ignore it. 'I'm feeling tired, maybe another time.' She remained at the foot of the lounge so her back was to the door. She knew it was seven steps to the front door.

He spotted the small liquor cabinet with two bottles in it. 'I know what we need.' He went over to the cabinet and eyed off the stockpile. 'Hm …' He looked at the half-empty bottle of scotch and Midori. 'Scotch it is then.' He grabbed two glasses and poured two large shots. He walked over to where Starlah stood frozen and shoved a glass at her.

She stared at it as though it were a foreign object. She tilted her head and frowned at him. Was he being serious? Why the hell would she want to have a drink with him when the reason he was told to drive her home in the first place was because she already had too much?

When she didn't take the glass, he placed both glasses onto the glass coffee table. It chinked as the two objects met. He stood back up and entered her space. Ripples of disgust washed over her at his close proximity.

'Come on, Starlah … chill out, will ya? I'm just trying to be nice.'

Her hand flew up to her throat and rubbed it nervously. 'Um, I don't feel like a drink, thanks though.' She swallowed hard. Her throat felt dry. She stepped back away from him and hoped he would take the hint and leave. Something clearly wasn't right.

He stepped behind her and grabbed her around the shoulders. 'Come on, relax, have a seat.' He massaged her shoulders as he propelled her forward and then pushed her down onto the sofa. He sat down next to her and grabbed her drink. 'One drink won't kill ya,' he sneered.

The hairs on her arms crept to attention. She couldn't work out why her body was screaming at her to run. In reality he'd never done anything to offend her; he'd always been attentive and caring towards Bella. He wasn't unattractive and Bella adored him. *So stop being such a drama queen. Just have a drink with the guy and then he'll leave.*

He picked up her hand and shoved the glass into it. She had no choice but to clasp her fingers around it. It felt like fire against her fingers.

'There you go ...' He picked up his glass and sipped on the liquid as he eyed her up and down.

Her stomach turned. She dreaded downing the liquid. Since her last attempt at trying to drown herself to death with alcohol, she tried to stay clear of anything resembling her dad's favourites, preferring to stick to the occasional white wine. She only had the scotch for visitors.

She closed her eyes and downed the amber liquid in one shot, hoping that would be enough for him to be done and leave. She shook her head as the liquid burned down her throat. A trickle of scotch dribbled down her chin.

'There you go. All good, see?' He leaned over and licked the trickle of scotch off her chin. 'Mm, tastes so good,' he purred.

She pulled back. 'Um Brad, I'm not too comfortable with this – you know, with Bella being my best friend and all.' *And the fact you repulse me.*

He leaned in again and whispered, 'So don't tell her then.' He licked her ear.

She shivered and pushed him away. 'OK, time for you to go.' She attempted to jump up to her feet to show him the door. She remained glued to the seat. He seized her by the wrist.

'Now now, where do you think you're going?' He calmly shook his head.

Her brain finally caught up to why her body was screaming at her. She was in trouble. She had hoped her instincts were wrong and all those weird bodily reactions were just because she was tired, but staring into his eyes she could no longer deny that. Her eyes watered. 'Please Brad. I'm tired, and I need you to leave.' She tried to pull her hand free.

He clasped it tighter. 'Well, I ain't ready to go, am I? You know what, Starlah?' He gritted his teeth. 'I'm bloody sick to death of you prancing around me, teasing me with your suggestive smile. And now you're playing frigid bitch.' He yanked her hand, forcing her to fall into his body.

She slammed into his chest and hit her cheek against his shoulder. It swelled up.

'Brad, you know this isn't right—please, just go.' *Fuck-fuck-fuck, why didn't she close the door on him?*

'Shut up,' he snapped at her. 'You can't get a bloke all heated up and then leave him hanging.' He squeezed his groin, emphasising his point. 'What am I supposed to do with this?'

She glanced down and could see his weapon bulging through his jeans. Her hands trembled. She looked away. Tears threatened to saturate her cheeks. Why the hell was he doing this?

'So you see my dilemma, Starbright …'

She spun her head around. 'Don't you dare call me that,' she spat between gritted teeth. 'You do not get to call me that.' She glared at him.

He crunched her hand. 'Really Starbright, I think I'll call you whatever I fuckin' want to.'

She stared into his cold piercing blue eyes and shook. There it was—the detached glare she remembered from her father's blank stares before he lost control. This was why he reminded her of her father. She had to close her eyes. She wanted to continue to pretend she didn't know what was coming.

He wrenched her up onto her feet. She stumbled and fell onto the floor, hitting her knee against the coffee table. She didn't dare cry out.

'I think it's time you showed me to your room.' He continued to drag her towards the bedroom. She tried to dig her knees, hands, feet, *anything* into the carpet, trying to hinder his progress. He pulled hard at her wrist, sending a loud popping sound around the room. This time she did cry out.

He snarled, picked up the remote for the CD player and switched it on. Loud enough to disguise her cries, but not loud enough to bring the police. Her favourite CD blared through the room.

'Now that should stop you annoying the neighbours with your pitiful cries.' He proceeded to drag her towards her bedroom.

He pulled her into the room and turned the light on, and they both stood in the doorway for a moment. He seemed to be catching his breath. She noted he had sprouted a sweat across his forehead. Must be hard work forcing someone to obey him. She glared at him. After a few heartbeats he shoved her hard, and she went flying onto the bed. She scampered across the bed towards the other side of the room. She stared at her bed and thought about what she had wished for that morning: for someone to be sharing her bed with her. She heard a small critical voice inside her head laugh. *Be careful of what you wish for.* Strangely it sounded a lot like her mother.

He paced the length of her room in front of the doorway, blocking her exit. She looked over towards the ensuite and contemplated trying to barricade herself behind the door.

She could smell her own fear; it oozed off her in waves. It smelt acid and primal. Her reptilian brain took over. She darted her eyes around the room, eyeing off potential escape routes. She felt an overwhelming need to flee. It was so strong that her legs vibrated with energy getting ready to propel her forward.

'Starlah, Starlah, Starlah. The all pretty, perfect, stuck-up bitch.' He continued to pace around erratically. His breath was irregular and forceful. His face burned with heat, rage and something she couldn't quite put her finger on. But that something she instinctively knew she should be afraid of.

Her brain switched gears, assessing that she wasn't able to flee; it searched her room for a weapon. It focused on the lamp, vase and maybe the CD player. She tensed her muscles and readied herself for action. She crept towards the vase. She tentatively reached her fingers out. She was a hands-breadth away.

He leapt over the bed towards her, lunged at her throat and grabbed tight. She fell backwards and hit her head against the wall, splitting the skin across the base of her skull. Blood splattered across the wall. It looked all too familiar. She froze. Her mind rationalised, *Stay still, do as he says and you'll get out of this.*

'Now see what you've made me do? All I wanted was to spend a nice romantic evening with you. I know you want it, all those suggestive looks you've been giving me.' He let her go and paced around again, running his fingers through his sweat-soaked hair. 'So why are you playing the frigid bitch now?' He stopped and stared down at her.

She couldn't believe he had misinterpreted all those *what the fuck?'* looks with an *'I want to fuck'* look. 'Brad, please stop this … Think about what Bella's going to say.' She slid up the wall, using her trembling hands and back to help her stand. As she stood her back smudged the blood splatter across the wall, smearing it into an artistic stroke, complementing the shade of her doona cover.

He snapped his head around and bore his eyes into hers. 'You say anything to Bells, and I'll do to you what that guy did to my mum.' He clenched his teeth and fists tight. His knuckles bulged white. He paced erratically lost in his tormented world.

Starlah swallowed hard. Did he just say what she thought he said? His mother was killed. A wave of ice trickled down her spine. Starlah knew about Brad's mum committing suicide when he was a toddler and had felt a strange connection with her. Or maybe it was gratefulness that she didn't succeed herself. She often explained away the differences between Bella and Brad by the fact that Brad was their dad's first child with another woman and Bella was the result of his second marriage. Otherwise she could never work out how the two were related.

Brad was four years older than Bella, and although you could see a few similarities with physical characteristics, his lack of any warmth and personality made him look severe. On the other hand, Bella's features and personality oozed warmth and joy.

There had been rumours about his mother's death, but the cops couldn't find enough evidence and had to conclude suicide. She stared at him and for a nanosecond felt sorry for him.

He muttered to himself, frantically running his hands through his hair. He looked like a rabid animal, unpredictable and dangerous.

'They thought I was too young to remember, but I can't ever remove that image from my brain.' He rubbed agitatedly across his mouth. 'They said an eighteen-month-old wouldn't be able understand what was happening.' He spun around and looked pleadingly into her eyes. 'Do you know what that does to a young boy?'

She shook her head, still clutching the wall for support. She could feel the blood trickling down her back, mixing with the ice taking up residence there.

He shook his head. 'I'll tell you what it does.' He stopped pacing, walked up to her face and stood a few inches away from her. 'It makes you stronger, that's what it does. I don't take shit from no one, and I don't take no for an answer.' He lifted his hand and ran his hot index finger across her cheek, gently at first, then he poked hard at her swollen cheek.

She flinched and tried to turn her head away. She couldn't bear having his demented glare imprinted on her retina forever. Bella's image danced through her mind. Did Bella know any of this? God, she so wished she didn't always listen to her. She quivered and her throat tightened. She could taste the alcohol burning up her throat. How the hell did her birthday surprise get to this point?

His face changed and took on a charming smile. 'So I'm going to try and make this easy for you. I ain't gonna ask, so you don't have to say no.' He spread his hands out to the side and faced them upwards.

She couldn't move, her body completely forgetting that it was capable of movement. She stared blankly at him, waiting for some sort of direction. He continued to stand in front of her and stare into her eyes, not even blinking. His hands went to his belt and fumbled with the buckle. It rattled as it came undone. He smirked. He unzipped his jeans, tormenting her with the zzz sound. It echoed around the room; she could hear it above the music.

Her heart pounded against her ribs with such force, she could literally feel it smashing against her ribcage. It palpitated as adrenaline surged through her bloodstream. She couldn't move her eyes; they were glued to his.

He leaned in and planted a forceful kiss against her lips, bruising them with the impact. His stubble burned against her skin. She squeezed her eyes and mouth shut tight, hoping to keep him out of her body.

He squeezed her jaw with his hand, forcing her mouth partially open, enough for him to shove his alcohol-impregnated tongue into her mouth. She couldn't breathe. *Fuck!*

He pinned her body with his against the wall. The remaining air in her lungs was squeezed out. She couldn't take another breath in. Panic bubbled through her heart and mind. It inched its way up through her body and out through her mouth. She let out a small, desperate scream.

He covered her mouth with his again, and her scream was sent through his mouth into the abyss. He pressed into her, rubbed his weapon against her and moaned. 'Yeah baby, you're a screamer, just the way I like it.' He buried his face into her hair and sucked in a deep, audible breath. 'So love that vanilla.'

She tried to break free. He grabbed both of her wrists and pinned them above her head with one hand. He used the other rough hand to slide up the side of her thigh and under her dress, landing his hand onto her buttocks, which he squeezed hard. He continued to rub himself against her and sent haggard, heaving breaths into her ear.

'Please Brad, please please, stop …' She couldn't hold back the tears. They cascaded down her cheeks in torrents. She choked on his saliva and her own tears. She gagged and spat.

Her legs gave way and she would have crumbled to the floor if he weren't pinned up against her. He must have felt her slump, he spun her around and shoved her onto the bed. It protested and squeaked.

She laid face down, sprawled across the bed. The way she landed sent her dress up over her buttocks, revealing her body. He jumped onto her back, slamming his knee into her, and she cried out.

He positioned himself so he straddled her back, pinning her to the bed. He leaned into the back of her head and tugged on her bloodied hair, pulling her head up. 'Yeah baby, that's it—take you from behind.' He stuck his wet tongue into her ear.

She sobbed, coughed and gagged all at once.

He manoeuvred himself down her body so he could use his

knees to force her legs apart. His breath was hot and ragged against her ear; she shivered. He writhed against her back.

'No–no–no! Please stop, Brad … please, please, please.' She could feel him fumble with his jeans, and then his weapon was freed against her skin.

He tugged at her underwear until it ripped and fell away, no longer protecting her from him. He slid down further and lined himself up for the assault. She felt him hovering between her legs. Her body clenched and tried to retract away from him. She couldn't move.

'I know you want this.' He kissed the side of her neck.

She closed her eyes and gritted her teeth, and then she saw her safe room in the distance. *Thank God.* She exhaled, detached and drifted off to her safe room, the one she used to visit whenever her parents went too far. She was no longer a part of this.

WHILE IN HER safe room the strangest thing happened; she felt him being yanked off her and slammed into the wall. Brad yelled in surprise. She took in a delicious, deep breath. From her safe room she watched in awe as a tall, dark-haired man with amazing blue eyes pin Brad up against the same wall she had been pinned up against.

She clutched her pink teddy and continued to watch from the safety of her secret room as the figure squished Brad's head into the wall. She thought he was going to push his skull all the way through.

Brad yelled out, 'Get the fuck off me, man.' He tried to push back.

The tall, angry man looked like he was going to rip Brad a new one. She giggled – a new one. Wouldn't that be funny?

The wall cracked with the force of Brad's head being shoved into it. He screamed again.

'You touch her again and I won't stop next time. You got it?' he spat into Brad's face.

Brad recoiled. 'OK, I won't touch her again. Just get the fuck off me.'

The man yanked Brad from the wall and shoved him hard towards the door. Brad stumbled and fell and scampered forward on his hands and knees, clutching his jeans. He ran out the door.

Her mysterious saviour came up to her and gently touched her face. She didn't move. 'Starlah, are you all right?' He sat down next to her on the bed.

She stared blankly at him, not fully registering his presence. She was still in her safe room. He gently stroked her hair back and studied her swollen face. He looked pained, his brows knitted together.

'Oh Starlah, why the hell don't you ever listen? I did try to warn you, but as usual you ignored me.' His jaw clenched tight, but his eyes were soft. They actually glowed, as a matter of fact; he seemed to glow all over. 'Starlah—Starlah, can you hear me?' He gently shook her.

She continued to stare at him, not moving, just breathing.

He leaned in and hugged her against his warm, comforting chest. 'My love please, it's me.' He rocked her soothingly.

She melted into his body, which was strong and warm and safe. He was safe. He – who was he? She looked up into his face and frowned. She couldn't place him. He did seem familiar. Did she know him somehow? His eyes, she knew those eyes. The memory filtered through her mind and banged on her safe room door. It's OK; you can come out now, it beckoned to her.

'Ardaleigh?' she croaked.

'Yes my love, it's me.' He hugged her tight in relief. 'You had me so scared. Are you all right?' He looked down into her eyes.

Her mind was in a fog. The adrenaline dump dispersed through her body. Fragmented consciousness filtered through. 'Ardaleigh, are you really here? I thought I had dreamt you.' She continued to stare at him, struggling to make sense of what had just happened.

He gave a nervous laugh. 'Yeah, I know, that's what you were supposed to think.' He stroked her hair. 'I'm not permitted to show my physical self to your world.' He looked pained again. 'But I just couldn't—' He darted his eyes around the room, staring at the blood and scattered pieces of her life. 'I couldn't watch him destroy you like that—I just couldn't,' he whispered the last words.

She continued to rest her face against his chest and stared up at his glowing face. She felt sedated by his presence. Everything felt surreal, as though she was watching from afar. Her eyes travelled down and spotted the pendant hanging off his neck; it looked familiar. It looked like the other half of her pendant, the one that Daniel had given to her. She reached up and touched it. It was warm and vibrated against her fingers, as did hers when she first touched it.

'I don't understand; why do you have this?' She twirled his pendant around, catching the light off it.

'It seems your brother is much better at listening to me than you are,' he said. 'It's a twin flame. They were made from the same source and always belong together.' He continued to caress her hair.

Was he just talking about the pendant? She looked back up into his eyes. 'What do you mean—the same source?'

'Starlah, I've said enough already. Just know that they belong together.' He leaned in and pressed his soft lips against her forehead, sending ripples of energy through her body, reminiscent of the kiss she thought she had dreamt back when she tried to end it all.

Her heart quickened. Her mind allowed the cloud to lift. Her fingers trembled. Panic bubbled up from the pit of her stomach. She darted her eyes around the room. 'What happened?'

He clutched her tight. His brows were just about fused together. 'I wish I could protect you from this world's heartache. I have been sent to watch over you, yet I am not allowed to interfere with your life. How am I supposed to stand by and watch them destroy you?' His body vibrated and glowed brighter.

His energy seeped into her body, pulsing through her bloodstream. She felt immense love and power. She looked back up into his eyes. They shimmered like blue streams; her breath was caught mid-exhale. 'What are you?' she whispered. 'Are you an angel?'

He laughed. 'No, not quite. I haven't quite made it to that level, but I am not of this world. However, I do have the privilege of watching over you.' He darted his eyes around the room. 'I hope I am allowed to continue to do so after this event.' He swallowed hard.

His whole body shimmered, looked transparent and seemed to be disappearing right in front of her. The panic rose higher up her body. 'No, don't go, please don't leave me,' she said, as she tried to clutch what remained of his body.

He abruptly turned his head towards the door and stared as though he was listening to something. 'I must leave now.' He kissed her sweetly on the side of her head. 'I love you.' And with that he was gone, leaving her in the wake of his absence again.

She rummaged her hands through her doona as though he had simply been shrunken and was lost in there somewhere. 'Ardaleigh,' she sobbed. She darted her eyes around her room and took in the blood and mess. She froze as the memory of Brad filtered through. Her body heaved in fast, deep gasps.

'Starlah … Starlah, where are you?' She heard someone yell from outside. She darted her eyes towards the door and waited.

The panicked voiced called out again, 'Starlah?'

She stumbled to her feet, recognising the voice and edged her way towards the door. Her face throbbed. The back of her skull had clotted over, and the blood had matted her hair. She willed her body forward. It ached from deep within. She managed to reach the doorway, grabbing it for support.

'Shit, Starlah. What the hell happened to you?' Daniel ran to her.

She stood in the doorway with her arms out to the sides. Her dress hung off her in pieces, her hair was splayed around her. A wave of horror crashed through her and her body convulsed. No longer able to contain the panic, she allowed it to boil forth. It spewed out in heaving sobs that rocked her to the core. Her legs gave way and she crumbled to the floor.

Daniel ran to her, catching her as she fell into his arms. She clutched at him with desperation, sobbing into his body. He cradled her, his eyes searching the room. 'What the hell happened?'

She couldn't talk. All she could get out was … 'Brad.'

His body clenched. 'That bastard did this to you?' She could feel his fury through his body. 'I'll fuckin' kill him.' He gripped her tight. 'I'll fucking crush him.'

YOUNGER BROTHER, you have been summoned by your Bludlin Guild; for what reason do you know?' Katalin asked.

Ardaleigh stood in the centre of the temple's illuminated room, facing six of the Harper Elders. Each initiate such as himself was born into a particular Bludlin, and that Bludlin had its own guild responsible for educating, guiding and disciplining its members. Ardaleigh swallowed hard. He knew this meeting would be for discipline.

'Yes, Elder Sister.' He looked up into the shimmering blue eyes of Katalin. They held compassion and understanding. He lowered his eyes. 'I have breached the law of our nature.' He folded his hands in front of him in surrender. He hated disappointing the elders, but Starlah's bruised face haunted him.

'You do remember the law of the Fourth Realm; do you not, Younger Brother?' Tomace said, looking down upon Ardaleigh with a stern look as he floated above on his ascended throne. His brown hair glistened with the light above, but his turquoise eyes darkened as they stared at him through his knitted brows.

'Yes, Elder Brother.' Ardaleigh kept his face lowered as he recalled that which he had learnt many aeons ago. 'Although we may interface with the subject's subconscious we may never disclose our light bodies or manifest them in the Third Realm physically.' Ardaleigh resented having to recite the Code of Comportment.

'Ah, I see you have not forgotten our laws, young Bludlin,' Eldest Brother Harper interjected as he walked into the temple's domain and faced Ardaleigh with a warm smile.

Ardaleigh looked up into his sovereign's glowing face and smiled. He always felt love and respect for the head of the Harper's Bludlin. Each guild of the land, and there were many, had its own leader. Each initiate belonged to his own soul's bloodline. Ardaleigh belonged to the Harper Bludlin.

The other elders cast their eyes down as Eldest Brother made his way to his throne. His white translucent gown billowed around him. He eased himself into his chair, and it autonomously ascended to join the others in mid-air. He waved his hand in front of him. 'As you were.'

'Thank you, Eldest Brother. As I was saying to our young brother here, the law of our land must be upheld.' Tomace continued to give Ardaleigh a stern look. He had always displayed intolerance when dealing with Ardaleigh. The two had been friends many lifetimes ago. Tomace had ascended after his last life cycle and now felt the need to assert his 'wisdom' upon his younger brother. 'So Younger Brother, do you know what the consequences are for continued disregard of our laws?'

'Yes,' Ardaleigh whispered, knowing that repeated violation of the Fourth Realm's law could result in rebirth. He felt his heart squeeze. If he was reborn into Starlah's world as a newborn then he would have to wait a whole lifetime before the two of them could be together again. And that was only if the Harper Guild deemed him and her atoned.

Starlah's forced rebirth left Ardaleigh heartsick. He had pleaded with his Guild to allow him to be her guardian. Eventually, the Eldest Brother succumbed and granted him guardianship of her just in time to stop her taking her own life at the age of seventeen. If she had succeeded their reunion would have been hindered for many life cycles. He couldn't bear to be removed from her for one lifetime, let alone many.

'What do you have to say for your actions, Younger Brother?' Katalin looked down with consideration.

Ardaleigh looked up pleadingly and whispered, 'She is my flame, Elder Sister.' He cast his eyes down so they couldn't see them water. 'She is my one and only, and my heart breaks every time hers does.' He fell to his knees. 'I plead lenience with your disciplining, my Harper Bludlin. I beg forgiveness and ask that I may continue to watch over her.' Prostrating himself he rested his head on the floor and awaited his elders' deliberation.

The elders' bodies turned translucent as they closed themselves off from Ardaleigh. They murmured above him in their secret language and debated, deciding his fate. His stomach clenched in anticipation.

Starlah's warm eyes stared through his mind. How he longed to get lost in them again. Her sensual lips beckoned to him from the past. His body shimmered with the memory of how they felt against his own. He squeezed his eyes tight. The pain in his soul was too much to bear at times. The longing he felt for his twin flame burned through him. He felt as though he would literally combust. He would have to learn how to channel his passion more constructively, as Elder Sister Katalin implored.

He hoped that the elders could see into his heart and know that he had done his best to get Daniel there on time, but what was he supposed to do, let her be destroyed? No, she had suffered enough at the hands of her parents. He couldn't turn his back on her. It devastated him that he hadn't been able to protect her from her parents, and he wasn't going to let Brad violate her like that. Now he prayed that wasn't beyond forgiveness.

'Younger Brother Ardaleigh, please stand so you may be initiated with wisdom.' Eldest Brother Harper's voice boomed through his mind.

Ardaleigh jumped to attention. 'Yes, Eldest Brother. I am ready for whatever you have deemed necessary.' As he awaited the lightning bolt of wisdom to be transcribed through him Starlah's beautiful face smiled at him. He held his breath as the energy of the seven masters pulsated through his being. He collapsed to the floor, absorbing aeons of wisdom. He hoped at the end of the lesson he still found himself as Starlah's guardian.

SEVEN

STARLAH STUMBLED out of Daniel's room towards the living room. She couldn't remember having been taken there. She felt groggy. Did he slip her something when he offered her a drink? She looked at her watch; it was 2:12 pm. She couldn't believe she had been asleep for hours.

At some point he must have changed her out of her ripped clothes and put her into someone's nightie. It didn't look like anything she owned and she figured that even if he was into wearing nighties, it wasn't his size. Danny must have a girlfriend … weird. She still pictured him as that geeky fifteen-year-old.

She walked up behind him. 'Hi.'

He was facing the window, looking out into the front yard. He seemed lost in his own world, clutching a glass. He spun around when he heard her words. 'Hey, how are you feeling?'

She saw him cringe when he saw her bruised face. He squeezed the glass tight, then downed the liquid and looked away. His jaw twitched.

She hadn't looked into the mirror, but she figured she didn't look too good. 'I'm OK,' she lied, walked up to him and hugged him, resting her head against his back.

He turned and hugged her tight. She could feel his rage still burning through his body. She had never seen him so wild.

'I'm glad,' he said.

She let him go. He pulled away, walked back over to the bottle sitting on top of the kitchen bench and poured himself another drink. He turned and held the bottle up to her. 'Do you want one?' he asked.

She shook her head.

He turned back around and placed the bottle down with force. She jumped at the sudden bang. He walked over to the three-seat red leather sofa and sat down, not seeming to know what to do or say.

She stood back and stared at him as he sipped on the liquor. Her body felt raw and weak, as though she had been through an UFC ring. She couldn't get Brad's image out of her mind or the taste of his tongue out of her mouth. She kept gagging on and off. She folded her arms around herself, bracing herself against the memory.

'So, do you live here on your own?' She broke the silence.

He looked back up at her. 'Yeah, but Sara hangs out here most weekends.' He looked back down into his lap, swirling his glass.

'Is she your girlfriend?' She walked over to the other side of the sofa and sat down.

'Yeah, Sara's pretty cool, been together for eighteen months.' He frowned and swallowed hard. He shook his head. 'I want to go smash his head in. I can't sit here and pretend nothing's happened.' He looked out the window.

'I know, but I just want to forget about it—and I don't want you to get in trouble.' She fought her tears, trembling.

'Yeah, that's the problem. I'd probably go too far.' He swallowed the alcohol and wiped his hand across his mouth. 'Been there, done that.' He raised the glass in salute to his past.

'What do you mean?' She stared at him, afraid of his answer.

'Where do you think I've been all those years? I would have come for you if I could, and when I could I didn't think you want to hear from me.' He frowned and stared at the empty glass.

'What—what do you mean?' She rubbed her throat.

He sighed and looked up at her. 'When I was seventeen I broke into a hardware store with a couple of mates. We planned on robbing the place but ran into a security guard.' He hesitated, 'You gotta understand, I was a different person then. Dad had me so enraged at him and the whole world …' He placed his face into his hand and shook his head. 'I beat that poor man to an inch of his life. I got five years for that.' He lifted his face and waited for her to respond.

She could see the pain written across his face, but she couldn't open her mouth. She simply stared at him.

He looked away. 'Anyway. I'm different now.'

She moved closer and grabbed his empty hand. 'I understand. It's all right, Daniel. That's why you can't get involved.'

He gritted his teeth. 'He can't get away with this.' His face burned. 'At least go to the cops.'

Starlah's phone beeped. She stared at it.

'Are you gonna check that?' he said.

She shook her head fast. 'No, it's probably Bella again. She's already left seven messages and rung twice.' She closed her eyes. 'I just can't face her yet.'

'Yeah, you should tell her about her psycho brother.' Daniel jumped up and grabbed her phone, scrolling through her messages. 'Huh right, she's concerned about her fucking mental case brother, says he came home ranting about some punk threatening him, packed a bag and took off. She wants to know what the hell happened when he left with you. What punk is he fucking talking about?' He looked at the phone in rage.

Starlah was afraid he was going to throw the thing against the wall. She thought back and remembered something she had forgotten. 'How did you know I was in trouble and where I live?'

'What are talking about? You texted me, saying "SOS" and your address.' He frowned at her. 'Don't you remember texting me that?'

She closed her eyes and thought back. Did she send that message? No, she hadn't been in a position to make any calls or texts. Her mind continued to scroll through the night's events until he filtered through. Her breath halted when she saw his eyes in her mind. She snapped them open and grabbed her pendant. It was warm and comforting.

'What?' Danny looked at her.

'Nothing, I was having a flashback.' She caressed the pendant, sensing him close by. Her heart fluttered with the memory of his handsome face and his protective presence. *Ardaleigh,* she spoke to him in her mind, hoping that he would be able to hear her. *Please Ardaleigh, answer me. Give me some sort of sign that you are still with me.* When he didn't answer her heart sank—despair's heavy cloud descended upon her.

Daniel looked over at her, and she trembled. He walked over, sat down next to her and wrapped his arms around her. She allowed the tears to flow freely, drenching his T-shirt with years of heartache. He gently rocked and soothed her hair. 'It's gonna be OK. I'll look after you – promise.'

She couldn't talk; she had a lifetime of tears boarded up in her heart. The dam seemed to have split open and was pouring out all over her and Daniel. She just hoped that at some point it would stop.

EIGHT

STARLAH TOSSED and turned in her sleep. She was exhausted, yet a sound sleep eluded her. The past month had been one torturous round of therapy after another. She couldn't believe she let Daniel talk her into seeing Sara's cousin, who was a psychologist specialising in abuse cases.

She couldn't believe she was actually one of those cases. Sure, she knew her parents were pretty messed up, but she never identified herself as being abused. That's how bloody good they had been at making her feel like she deserved what they dished out.

Unfortunately once the tears erupted they didn't want to dry up. The hour-long sessions twice a week were wearing her out, but they gradually chipped away at the scab sealing tight the festering wounds of her childhood as well as helping her deal with Brad's assault. She struggled with admitting to herself that she still had anger towards Daniel for leaving.

Daniel was a complete life saver. His devoted support and comfort gave her the permission and space to cope with the overload of emotions flooding her brain and nervous system. So how was she supposed to admit that his betrayal still rocked her?

Well, she couldn't. That would be for another time. Besides, it wasn't his fault, he had suffered at the hands of their parents more than she had. Then he got into the wrong crowd and was locked up. So really, it wasn't in his control. Right?

She nodded, happy with that analysis. But she couldn't say she was happy with what had been behind the bolted-up door in her subconscious. Once the door was shattered with the aid of Brad's birthday surprise things poured out in torrents. Her body shut down. She couldn't eat, sleep or face seeing anyone except Daniel and her therapist. She even quit her job as an admin officer in a public hospital. Bella and Jaz kept trying to track her down. They left frantic messages every day.

Daniel had responded to both of them with a brief message telling them she needed some time out and would contact them when she was ready. Starlah hoped he hadn't added anything about Brad to Bella's message.

Now she lay in her bed, being tormented for the millionth time. Her mind drifted through Nightmare Land; her body quivered. The usual greeted her. Her dad's face interchanged with Brad's. It didn't matter whose face it was; the effect of their presence in her mind was the same.

She flipped over, kicking off the doona. Sweat saturated her body. She groaned as the image of a magnified monster's claw descended upon her, ripping her skin from her body. At this point she usually bolted upright in her bed, screaming.

Ardaleigh's face evaporated the nightmare with a single swipe of his smile. He appeared vividly in her mind's eye. His eyes twinkled through the bridge between her world and his.

'Hi beautiful,' he said.

Her heart raced, this time not because of the nightmare. 'Ardaleigh, oh my God. I thought you were gone forever.' Tears flowed freely. Her body hugged the pillow.

In her dream she ran to him and threw her arms around him. He felt solid and so real. She looked down at herself. She didn't recognise her body. It was more mature and beautiful. She felt brimming with life. She looked up at him, his eyes pouring love into her, completely filling her with aeons of shared moments.

'My beloved, how I have missed you,' he leaned in and whispered against her ear.

She reached up and touched his glowing pendant. It vibrated and hers vibrated in unison against her chest. Her physical body in its sleeping state reached up and grabbed her pendant. It hummed against her hand.

She couldn't shake the feeling this wasn't a dream. It all felt so real. 'Ardaleigh, what is this place?' She inhaled his essence.

He ran his hand through her silken hair, pulling it off her face. He gazed into her eyes for a few moments and then smiled. 'This is what some call the astral world. It has also been referred to as a bridge between our two worlds.'

'Oh–wow–it does seem familiar. Have I been here before?'

She looked around the golden-hued room. There wasn't any

furniture in the room and no walls. The backdrop appeared as a mirage, blending beautiful soft pink and mauve colours. If she strained her eyes she thought she could make out patterns of trees and buildings in the distance. It was confusing to her senses. One moment when she was lost in his eyes the room seemed solid and contained, but then when she shifted her gaze the room became a mirage again.

He caressed her cheek. 'Many times, over many lifetimes. We have shared many loving moments here when our life journeys have taken us in different directions.'

'Hm, so does that mean this is real? That you're real and not some wonderful dream I'm having?' She melted further into his strong arms.

'My love, this is the only thing that's real. Our love is the one thing you can always believe in.' He teased her with his eyes, drawing her in. She held her breath. Her body tingled, every nerve ending alight with desire and passion. He inched closer. Her heart trembled with the anticipation of their reunion. He closed his eyes, lowered his face to hers and breathlessly whispered, 'Please remember the reason for your rebirth so you may return to me, my love.'

He pressed his soft, warm lips against hers, causing an explosion through her body. Their two bodies intertwined, blazing into a flame, exploding through time and space. There was no longer individuality. The two of them merged into a blissful flame of energy.

Starlah sat bolt upright in her bed, clutching her pendant. It burned into her palm. She let it go. She was gasping and seemed to be aglow with energy. She darted her eyes around the room, feeling exposed as though she had been caught with her clothes off in public.

'What the hell was that?' She continued to pant. His eyes burned through her mind. She ran her finger across her lips, feeling his warmth against them. Her fingers trembled. 'Ardaleigh?' She drew in a deep breath, trying to fill her lungs with his memory. A light tingling swept across her left cheek. She closed her eyes, picturing his lips there. Was that her name she heard whispered in the breeze?

Confusion rocked her senses. She felt as though her anchor to this world had been uprooted and now she drifted precariously between the two worlds. His image continued to glow through her heart and mind. He felt so real to her.

He is real, she affirmed, as was her other self, more real than anything she ever felt in this world. But was that even possible? How could any of that be possible? She shook her head. Even though her head couldn't make sense of it her heart knew the truth. And now that it did how was she to carry on as though nothing had changed?

She clutched her sheets, feeling divided. Not knowing whether to get up or go back to sleep. If she went back to sleep would he be there to greet her? She hoped so although the intensity of their bodies exploding into a single flame scared the hell out of her.

She heard Daniel rustling in the kitchen and felt relieved. Maybe she should keep her feet in this reality for now. She had to admit the other one rattled her. Deciding that getting up was her best option she jumped up and stumbled, feeling giddy. Having one foot in each realm wasn't conducive to walking straight. She straightened her back and scrunched her shoulders up and down a few times, taking slow, deep breaths.

She walked along the hallway, holding onto the walls. She stumbled around the corner and cleared her throat. 'Morning.' She grabbed the kitchen bench for support. She cast her eyes down, trying to hide the heat in her cheeks. She hoped she hadn't made any moaning sounds while she engaged in her dreamtime rendezvous. How mortifying would that be?

'Hey sleepy head, morning.' Daniel flipped a pancake, looked up into her face and smiled.

She continued to stand at the kitchen bench and studied him. 'Mmm, smells good.' He didn't appear to have noticed anything.

'Glad you're feeling up to some old favourites.' He flipped the pancake onto a plate and pushed it her way.

For the first time in weeks she actually had an appetite and grabbed the plate, ready to drown the pancake with strawberries and maple syrup.

'Cuppa?' he asked with his hand over the kettle.

She smiled, shoving a piece of dripping pancake into her mouth. 'Sure, fill her up.'

Her 'Ardaleigh afterglow' seemed to be infectious, and Daniel seemed particularly upbeat this morning. It appeared as though the heavy, sad cloud between them had evaporated.

He glanced at her between flips, looking as though he was holding back a chuckle. 'So. You look rested.' The corner of his lip curled.

Was that a hint of teasing?

She ran her fingers across her pendant; it had cooled down. 'Actually yeah, I feel pretty good.' She let a giggle escape, still in amazement at her morning interlude.

He laughed in return. 'Cool,' he said, finishing up breakfast.

Oh my God, maybe he had heard her.

She cast her eyes down as she sipped on her coffee, allowing the heat from the cuppa to explain her flushed cheeks. He remained coy, continued to play the dutiful kitchen hand and cleaned up the morning mess, smiling as he washed up.

S TARLAH TRIED not to look for too long at herself in the mirror as she applied foundation under her eyes, trying to conceal the dark patches living there. She seemed to have aged in the last two months. Her eyes looked like they belonged to someone who had seen the truth of life.

She was procrastinating. She didn't know how she was going to tell Jaz what happened. She traced around her lower eyelids with charcoal eyeliner, hoping to disguise the pain.

Jaz's persistent ringing and texting loosened Starlah's resolve on her self-imposed exile. She caved and agreed to meet up with her. She still couldn't bear to see Bella. How do you tell your best friend what her brother really was?

She peeled herself away from her tormented image and made her way out the door. Her heart raced in anticipation. How was Jaz going to react? Would she believe her or doubt her sanity?

She couldn't bear to see her friend retreat in doubt or disgust.

She knew that the disgust belonged to Brad, but she couldn't help but feel ashamed. Maybe she had led him on. Maybe there was something about the way she behaved towards him that suggested he could do that to her.

Her therapist explained that it was normal for her to feel these things, but they were false internalisations of her responsibility. He was the monster, not her. That was a hard one to accept, especially since her parents had trained her to accept that she was always to blame.

Jaz sat by the window, sipping on a coffee as Starlah entered the coffee shop. She looked up and smiled. Starlah managed to smile in return. It was good to see her. She had grown her short cropped hair so it was feathery, and she had changed the colour to a more subtle warm blonde.

'Hey there,' she said, beaming.

'Hi Jaz, how are you?' Starlah sat down beside her and fidgeted with her hands.

'Nice to finally catch up. I've missed you.' Jaz stared into her eyes.

Starlah looked away. She was afraid Jaz would be able to read her. 'Yeah, you too.' She looked down at her hands and realised they were trembling. There was a pause between them. 'Do you want another coffee?' Starlah asked as she jumped up, clutching her purse.

'I'm good, thanks.' Jaz eyed her with concern.

Starlah headed to the counter and took a deep breath, relieved for the moment's grace. A young woman walked past wearing the vanilla perfume she used to love. The smell sent her right back to that night. Her subconscious brain couldn't separate the two moments and was screaming at her to run. An internal quiver rocked her whole body and squeezed her throat. She couldn't breathe; her heart bounced around, sending adrenaline into her bloodstream. Her mind chanted, *Run. Get out now. Run.*

The barista behind the counter stared into her face. 'Well, do you want cream with that or not?'

She looked up into his frowning eyes and realised that he had been talking to her. 'Um sure, thanks.' She looked down into her purse and struggled co-ordinating her hands to fish out coins to pay. She could see out of the corner of her eye that he had rolled his eyes at her. *Oh God, help me get through this.* She willed her body to behave.

Starlah returned to the seat next to Jaz and took a deep breath. For a moment she stared out the window at the kids walking past, and when they were no longer in view she exhaled and faced her. 'So, um, I have something to tell you,' she barely managed to whisper.

'Yeah, I figured that much. Starlah, whatever it is you can tell me.' Jaz looked reassuringly into her eyes. She put her coffee down and placed a warm hand on top of Starlah's cold one.

'So after my birthday you know how Brad drove me home …' She struggled to spit out his name. Mentioning it caused a physical response in her stomach.

Jaz nodded in confirmation and encouragement.

'Um, so he invited himself in and—' She squeezed her eyes

shut as the image of his cold eyes bore into her. Jaz squeezed her hand tighter. She extracted strength from it and continued, '—he pretty much tried to rape me.' She gave voice to the nightmare that had haunted her since that traumatic day.

Jaz stiffened, her hand squeezing Starlah's with force. After what felt like minutes she exhaled and slumped back in her chair. Her hand fell off Starlah's and hung limply in her lap. 'What the fuck?' She shook her head vehemently.

Starlah dropped her eyes to her hands, which were still rattling in her lap. Tears threatened to join the show. 'Um yeah, what the fuck for sure,' she mumbled, feeling drained. Silence sat between them for a while.

Jaz stared out the window and continued to shake her head. After a while she leaned forward and grabbed her hand again. 'Oh my God, are you OK? I just can't believe it. I always knew there was something seriously mental with that guy.'

Starlah exhaled in relief; she hadn't lost her friend. Tears trickled down her cheeks. 'Yeah, me too.' She nervously smiled as she swiped at them and darted her eyes around the coffee shop, hoping no one was watching.

'Well, that kinda explains everything. Did you go to the cops?' Jaz frowned.

Starlah shook her head. 'Couldn't.' She raised her shoulders. 'Couldn't do that to Bella.'

'Man, that's just so—fucked up.' Jaz struggled to find any other word, and given the fact she rarely swore those words said it all. The doorbell tinkled as someone entered. Jaz darted her eyes towards the approaching person. 'Oh shit, Starlah. I'm so sorry. I forgot I asked Bella to meet us here. I had no idea what was going on with you, sorry.' She grimaced.

Starlah's heart dropped to her stomach; she wasn't ready for this. She clutched her pendant to extract strength from it. It hummed against her skin and she felt a wave of calming energy disperse through her body, relaxing her muscles and calming her fragile heart.

'Oh Starlah, why the hell have you been hiding from us?' Bella threw her arms around Starlah, knocking her back in the chair.

Starlah laughed despite herself and hugged her back. She'd missed her flamboyant friend. 'Um, had some shit to sort out with the family. You know how it is.' She darted her eyes towards Jaz.

Jaz nodded and smiled reassuringly.

Bella took a seat and whizzed her eyes around the room. 'Where are these waiters?' She pouted her lips.

'You have to go up and order.' Jaz laughed.

'Oh right, it's one of those places.' She jumped out of her seat and walked towards the counter.

Starlah rubbed her throat. 'I'm not ready to tell her yet. OK?' she beseeched Jaz.

Jaz shook her head. 'I reckon you should tell her and the cops. But OK, I'll keep quiet.'

They both watched Bella order her coffee while she flirted with the cute guy behind the counter. Starlah swallowed hard. She hated hiding things from her friend, but what could she do? Brad was Bella's brother and her loyalty would always be with her family. Starlah had decided that she would put the whole ordeal behind her and move on.

'OMG, how adorable is that guy?' Bella gushed as she took her seat. She smiled at her new friend and gave him a flirty little wave.

He smiled and waved back as he prepared her coffee.

'His name is Jake and he is twenty-two, and a muso. He works here to pay his bills but hopes one day to make it big with his music.' Bella relayed all the goss she extracted. She had that special quality that guys just gush over and confess all to. Both girls giggled—typical Bella.

When Bella was finished with her waving and smiles she redirected her attention to Starlah. Her eyes turned serious. Starlah's heart leapt to her throat.

'So Starlah, I think it's about time you 'fess up what's really been going down with you.' Bella stared into her eyes. There was something severe glaring through them.

Starlah sipped on her frappé and stared at the ring of condensation her cup left on the table. 'Huh?' she feigned ignorance.

'OK, enough of the bullshit. What the hell happened that night?' Bella scrunched her eyes.

Starlah had never seen her so intent and serious.

Jasmine darted her eyes nervously, from Starlah to Bella. 'Hang on, Bells. Ease up, will ya?' She leaned in and grabbed Bella's hand.

Bella pulled her hand away and continued to stare at Starlah. 'I want to know why my brother came home freaking out, blabbering incoherently and then disappears. We haven't heard from him since. So excuse me for wanting to know what happened.' She sat on edge, waiting for Starlah to answer.

Starlah's face heated up and tears welled. She didn't dare blink in case they spilled over the edge. She continued to stare down at the table. Why the hell did she agree to meet Jaz here? She regretted being such a pushover.

'Um well,' Starlah didn't have the right words for her. Whatever she said would be wrong.

'Leave her alone, Bella, it was your crazy brother's fault. He was the one that tried to rape her.' Jaz put her hand over her mouth. 'Shit, sorry Starlah.' She leaned back and held her mouth shut: too late.

Starlah darted her eyes first at Jaz and then at Bella. She held her breath as she watched her friend's face pale. Bella leaned back in her chair and stared at her. After a while she regained her composure and leaned forward.

'What are you saying? No way Brad would do anything like that.' She shook her head. 'You must have misinterpreted his actions.'

Starlah clutched her pendant; it transferred courage to her. 'No, it's hard to misinterpret being beaten up, having your clothes ripped off and being pinned down ready for assault.'

She gritted her teeth as anger seared through her veins. The boiling intensity surprised her. She thought she had dealt with it. She had spent hours convincing her therapist that she didn't feel any anger. But now as she struggled to hold in the anger-laden lava, she had to admit, maybe she should have spent more time dealing with it and less time deceiving her therapist and herself.

Bella and Jaz stared at her with their mouths open. After a while Bella jumped to her feet and looked out the window before turning towards Starlah. 'I don't believe you. I know my brother, and he is not the monster you're making him out to be.' She yanked up her designer bag, turned and stormed out of the coffee shop.

Starlah watched Bella leave and knew with certainty she had lost her best friend. Her heart crumbled. She stared at Jaz, her eyes pleading with her. They begged for her to not abandon her too. Her chin trembled, waiting for her to respond.

Jaz leaned forward and wrapped her hand around Starlah's trembling one. 'Don't worry. I'm not going anywhere,' she promised.

Starlah smiled and let the pool of tears trickle down her cheeks.

TEN

EXHAUSTION permeated every atom of Starlah's being. She stumbled through the front door to Daniel's place and willed her legs to move forward. It was moments like these she was grateful she took Daniel up on his invite to move in.

She had moved in since that night, giving up the rent on her place after two weeks. The idea of sleeping in that bed and spending silent moments staring at the wall her blood was splattered across rocked her. There was no way she wanted to be reminded of Brad every time she tried to go to sleep.

She ambled around the apartment, her hands shaking. Catching up for coffee had turned out to be way more draining than she hoped. Her body ached from the clenching of her muscles, and her heart mourned the loss of her best friend.

Closing her eyes only bought torment as Bella's rage burned

through her mind. She had never seen her so tormented. It was her fault, she supposed. If only she hadn't agreed to let Brad take her home or let him in he wouldn't have been tempted. And bloody Jaz blabbing, really, couldn't she just keep her mouth shut? But it was bound to get out sooner or later.

'Danny? You home?' her voice echoed through the apartment. No answer came. She clutched herself as the edges of the room seemed to squeeze in on her. A sweat had broken out across her forehead and she felt as though someone was watching her. She hoped it was Ardaleigh.

She clutched her pendant for the millionth time. It hummed sweetly against her fingers. An overwhelming urge to sleep enveloped her. She retreated to her room and dropped heavily onto the bed. As soon as her head sunk into the pillow she was teleported to another realm.

She stood in a temple. The walls illuminated golden hues across her face. She breathed in the sweetest smelling incense. It reminded her of spiced cinnamon. She darted her eyes around the spacious room, mesmerised by the beauty of the surroundings.

The walls were carved out of gold and silver, peppered with gems: rubies, sapphires and jade. She walked over and traced her fingers across a carved picture depicting floating figures above prostrated figures below. As soon as her fingers touched the warm, glorious wall a scene flashed before her eyes. She remembered herself being here many times before.

'Greetings, Younger Sister Starlah.'

Starlah jumped and spun around. As soon as her eyes met his the veil lifted, and she felt the need to fall to her knees. 'Oh,

Eldest Brother,' she cried, casting her eyes down in respect and gratuitous shame.

'You may stand.' He extended his hand so she could be helped to her feet.

As she rose she looked up into the Harper Elder's comforting smile and felt the overwhelming urge to embrace him, but held her childish needs to herself.

'Younger Sister, I embrace your essence.'

'As do I yours, Eldest Brother.' They touched foreheads in greeting, locking eyes for a moment.

'Ah yes, much heartache coursing through you, Younger Sister. I see your rebirth has propelled you into a difficult life.' He continued to read her spirit, his face echoing deep compassion and understanding.

Starlah stared into his eyes and felt the immense love being channelled her way. The pain and trembling from moments ago had evaporated and was replaced with warmth and revitalisation. 'Yes Eldest Brother, it is at times too much to endure.' She reflected on all the times she had attempted to do herself harm.

'Yes, I am pleased to see that those attempts failed. For the pain would not end with this life, Younger Sister.' He pulled his face away, walked over and sat on his cathedra. 'Come join me.' He waved his hand in front of him, directing her to the cushions on the floor.

Starlah followed her Sovereign's instructions and took her seat at his feet. She spread herself across several elaborately cross-stitched cushions depicting beautiful birds, butterflies and various flowers of this world. The colouring was vivid and lustrous, easily overshadowing the most radiant shades in the Third Realm.

Starlah maintained etiquette but felt relaxed in front of the Head of the Harper Guild. His presence encompassed all that resonated with love and wisdom. His essence, though he understood hate, rage and anger, did not embody those qualities.

The Harper Elder had been in existence before time, but his body depicted that of a man in his forties. His dark hair was peppered at the sides with silver streaks, and his vibrant azure eyes with amethyst specks held slight smile crinkles around them.

On the periphery of her mind Starlah caught glimpses of memories of how life evolved through the Fourth Realm, but she found it difficult as her conscious mind still perceived through the Third Realm, the two at odds with each other.

She stared down at her body. She couldn't believe it belonged to her. She never knew she could look so feminine and womanly. Her breasts were more prominent and soft. She wished she could take them back with her. She ran her fingers through her hair and noticed that it was longer, thicker and highlighted with golden copper tones. She wondered if her eyes matched the others of the Harper Guild: varying shades of iridescent blue, dispensing with her brown eyes.

'Younger Sister, I have summoned you for two reasons: foremost is the need to redirect you back on your life path. It appears you have become drenched in your life lessons and have become inert. A life journey was charted prior to your birth, one that I see has caused you much heartache and pain, but one that was of vital importance to ensure your reunion with your twin flame.'

He rubbed his chin. '*Which* brings me to the second reason: the dilemma we encounter with Younger Brother Ardaleigh. It seems our Young Bludlin is having trouble adjusting to your rebirth. He is on the verge of being propelled into a rebirth himself. I do not particularly wish to see this happen as I do not perceive it will evolve his spirit.' He looked into Starlah's eyes with intensity. 'And it may make your reunion improbable.'

Starlah's heart pounded at the mere mention of Ardaleigh's name and the impact of the Elder's words. Her heart contracted in pain, as she clutched her throat.

'His tumultuous heart is causing him to behave in a way that is attracting the attention of the Harper Bludlin Guild, and Tomace is petitioning for him to be rebirthed. So far I have allowed Ardaleigh to remain as he has promised not to interfere in your life again.' He looked down into Starlah's eyes. 'His heartache, however, is causing a ripple effect through the guild, and we can all feel the effects of his pain and desire for you. Hmm.' He stared out into the distance.

Starlah didn't know what to say. Being back in this realm illuminated how much she loved and longed for her twin flame. Her heart fluttered, and her skin begged for his caresses. She completely understood Ardaleigh's pain and longing. It really was torturous being forced apart.

'Yes, I see the pain and desire is mutual.' He smiled down at her knowingly. 'Younger Sister, as you are yet to gain the wisdom from your rebirth, I implore you, heed my words.' He closed his eyes and became translucent, sending waves of energy her way.

Starlah's body heated up and hummed with the vibration of the Harper Elder's energy. She closed her eyes and allowed the love to flow through her. She saw flashes of her life with her parents and the pain they put her through. She navigated through her life with her brother and friends and felt the love shared. She also saw and relived the night Brad tried to violate her. She witnessed all these events from a detached perspective.

The head of The Harper Bludlin opened his eyes and smiled down at Starlah with compassion. 'I know child, you do not yet see why it is you have been sent to live a life of such deep pain and heartache, but seek the day that it will make sense. When that transcendent day arrives you may re-join your Bludlin Guild and your twin essence. I beseech you achieve this enlightened state before there is no longer a possibility.'

He stood down off his cathedra and extended his hand for Starlah to stand. 'Until that time arrives you must live out the rest of your life without interference from Younger Brother Ardaleigh. This is why I am allowing the two of you to spend some time together before you return to your life.'

She nodded, unable to squeeze words from her tightening throat.

'Now, when you embrace Ardaleigh I implore you to try and soothe his heart and reiterate the need to allow you the free will to live your life without his interference. It is imperative you achieve your life's lesson through your own illumination.' He leaned into Starlah and placed his head against her forehead again. 'I embrace your essence.'

'As do I yours,' she managed to squeak out.

'Now go and see your Ardaleigh.' He smiled and walked out of the temple, leaving Starlah standing there trembling in anticipation.

ELEVEN

STARLAH WANDERED through the golden and emerald fields overflowing with vibrant red and pink ulander flowers. They reminded her of a cross between an orchid and poppy. Their stalks were the height of adult sunflowers, so she had to gently push her way through denser patches, enjoying the fragrant kisses they bestowed upon her skin.

She allowed her heart to navigate her way to him. She ambled gracefully, barefoot, allowing the gentle breeze and sunlight to bathe her skin with invigorating energy. It was like the whole of the Fourth Realm breathed in anticipation with her. That was the nature of this realm.

She gazed up at the breathtaking beauty of the aqua sky with light mauve highlighting the horizon as the sun headed towards the setting point and the two moons made their way in the sky. The setting of the sun took much longer to complete in the Fourth Realm.

There were many things about the Fourth Realm that resembled that of the third, like day and night. However, the Fourth Realm only had one season. The weather never deviated too much from being pleasantly warm, and the rain would fall as needed. It seemed the environment's consciousness was in tune with its residents' needs.

Starlah continued to bask in the glory of the setting sun, breathing in soothing, revitalising energy, recharging her body and mind.

'Greetings, Starlah.'

Starlah spun around at the intrusion. 'Elder Brother Tomace, what pleasure it is to greet you.'

'Yes, an unexpected surprise indeed. I am most perplexed by your appearance. There was no mention of such an occurrence at our last meeting. What grants your presence?' He lifted his chin.

Starlah studied his face and thought she detected scorn peering through his smile. She bit her lower lip, 'I think if Eldest Brother wished you privy to my summoning you would not be asking me. So even though I rejoice in your welcoming I must make my way to fulfil my duty.' She turned to leave. She didn't want to waste a single moment of her time with Ardaleigh, especially not on Tomace.

'Hmm, I think Ardaleigh's threatened rebirth has brought you here.' He goaded. 'An unusual breach of the regulation to allow you such a visit. It is just a visit, is it not? You haven't transcended your life's lesson and returned to us, have you?'

Starlah spun back around and glared at him. 'I think your

questioning needs restraint. My presence is of no concern to you. If you have further such need feel free to approach Eldest Brother and seek his counsel.' She gritted her teeth. She had forgotten how irritating Tomace's smugness could be.

'Ah, just a visit it is, then. Careful Sister, time may be running out for you and your twin flame. Your life's journey has an expiry date, and if you fail to transcend your life lesson this time you may not make it back to our Brother at all. Wouldn't that be a most unfortunate circumstance? My heart will mourn with you.' He bowed his head in false offering.

Starlah's heart shuddered at his words. Was time running out for her? What if she couldn't remember her life's plan? What if she failed, was lost to endless cycles of rebirth in other realms and never found her way back to her twin flame? She clutched her pendant. She wouldn't allow that to happen. She would do whatever it took to unveil her life path and ascend.

'Thank you Brother, for your encouraging words, but I must leave now.' Starlah turned and continued her way through the fields. She refused to allow Tomace to contaminate her heart and mind with his tormenting words and steal from her the joy that being in Ardaleigh's arms would bring.

The cascading of waterfalls welcomed her as she headed deeper into the vibrant fields. She instinctively knew she would find Ardaleigh by the stream. She shook off the remnants of Tomace's words and headed deeper into the meadow.

Her heart quickened. Her breath remained locked in her lungs. She forced herself to exhale and then inhale to bursting capacity, filling her lungs and mouth with the most enchanting scent. It triggered memories of love and complete surrender. She had arrived.

'Ardaleigh,' she whispered as she approached the shimmering aquamarine stream. She saw him before he noticed her. She stood back, taking in his muscular form. He was leaning his bare back against a large rock and was staring into the bubbling stream, his body bathed in the misty glow of the cascading waterfall. His body and face looked saddened and torn. Her heart ached for him. She wanted to run to him and soothe his pain with her lips.

She touched her trembling fingers against her lips and felt the heat there. Her pendant hummed against her chest, heating up as was her body. She noticed him clutching at his pendant. She saw his lips whisper her name. She couldn't bear the distance any longer. She floated towards him, unaware of her body moving.

He looked up into her smiling face and frowned. 'I must have lost my senses because you sure do look real.' He continued to stare into her face, not trusting his eyes.

'No, you're not that far gone. I'm here. Eldest Brother has summoned me here and is allowing us some moments alone.' She sat down beside him and leaned into his body, feeling his warmth and strength, her skin and heart alight with his presence.

'I just can't believe it.' He gently pushed her away so he could study her.

Starlah laughed, reached up and caressed his cheek. 'No, your eyes are telling you the truth. I really am here. It seems you have been causing some discordance amongst our Bludlin Guild.'

Her seductive fingers ran down his neck and across his smooth chest. Her fingers buzzed as they grazed across his firm, beautiful body … *Hmm.*

He grabbed her hand and brought it to his lips. He hovered, his lips glistening with hunger before searing them against her flesh, causing her to lose her breath. He pulled her into his body and sealed his lips against hers.

She fell into his arms, greedily pulling him into her body, wanting and needing him desperately. The frantic need she felt was almost painful.

He ran his hand through her hair, pulling her head back and kissing her deeply, his soft tongue exploring her mouth with tantalising precision. 'Oh Ardaleigh, I need you.' She gasped between breaths.

He pulled away and gazed into her teary eyes. 'And I you, Starlah, more than any words can say.' He ran his thumb across the side of her face and then across her parted lips. 'You are more beautiful than beauty itself.' His lips found hers again.

She giggled, loving his fluffy clichés. Her stomach flipped. 'You always did know how to make a girl feel desirable.' She trailed soft, feathery kisses from the corner of his lips across his neck and shoulder, lingering across his sculptured chest. She felt him quiver and inhale sharply.

'And you always did know how to ignite my body with your touch.' He traced his fingertips down her back and arms.

She shivered, her heart throbbing in her ears. Her face blazed with desire. She pulled away and faced him again before completely losing herself to his touch. 'Promise me something.'

'Mm, anything.' His eyes glazed over with yearning.

'Don't do anything that will cause you to be propelled into a rebirth. Please, Ardaleigh. Promise me,' she said.

He leaned in, kissing her as he whispered, 'I promise I will try.'

She smiled against his tormenting hungry lips. 'Typical Ardaleigh, master of word play.' She drew back and held his hands. 'You mustn't interfere in my life again, no matter how devastating or painful it may be. You know I was reborn to grow as a soul so we can finally be together for always.' She looked imploringly into his eyes. 'You must allow me the freedom to make my own mistakes and grow.' She squeezed his hands.

He looked down at her hands. 'I know that you are right, but it crushes me when you don't hear my whispers and heartache befalls you. You have no idea how soul shattering it is to watch your beloved endure such pain and be unable to prevent it or comfort her.'

She held his face. 'I know, my love. I know.' She held his eyes for a few moments and then stood and held out her hand for him. He allowed himself to be dragged to his feet.

'Where are we going?' He pulled at her hand.

She grinned. 'You'll see,' she said and continued to pull him towards the waterfall. She could feel the electricity building, and her breath quickened.

'Oh, that's where we're going.' He grinned, pleased with their destination.

The gentle showering of water droplets upon their heated skin felt like electrified kisses dancing across their bodies. Ardaleigh's eyes glowed brightly, and she imagined hers did in return. They reached the underpass to the waterfall and stood there for a few moments, staring into each other's eyes.

Starlah was the first to move. She unbuttoned her white cotton blouse and let it fall off her shoulders. He traced his eyes across her bare chest. She could see his chest rising faster. Her body tingled. She could feel the humming from behind the falls. She undid the string holding up her cotton pants and let it fall to the ground as well; she wasn't wearing underwear.

He dropped his white cotton pants in one swift motion. They stood there naked, bathing in each other's beauty.

'I embrace your essences, Ardaleigh.' She clasped his hand.

'As do I yours, Starlah.'

They turned and entered the Chamber of Resonance. The light from the crystals illuminated their path into the humming chambers. The vibrating echoes pulsed through their bodies. Every nerve ending was alight with tiny ripples of energy. Starlah's heart swelled with love.

They approached the centre of the chamber and stared into each other's eyes again. Goosebumps erupted across their bodies. 'Are you ready?' She smiled.

He nodded without taking his eyes off hers. They held hands and walked up to the iridescent clear quartz crystal platform that was surrounded by six other large, spiky forms of crystal, each representing the single form of the sacred seven – Melody's Stone. Surrounding the clear quartz platform were a large amethyst, lepidocrocite, smoky quartz, rutile, goethite and cacoxenite.

They lowered themselves onto the cool clear quartz platform, instantly alight with the vibrating energy entering their bodies, connecting with their base. They sat facing each other, knees touching, holding hands. 'I've so missed these moments. Your absence makes existing difficult.' Her lips no longer needed to move as their thoughts were connected with each other through the crystals within the chamber.

He didn't need to answer; she could feel everything he felt. The room flashed different hues as the resonance within the chamber attuned to their bodies. At first there was an unpleasant discord as Starlah had to raise her vibration from the Third Realm to accept the higher frequencies of the Fourth Realm, but after a few moments the sweetest harmonics swirled around the room and through their bodies.

Their bodies became attuned with the chamber's energy, and small pulses of energy flowed from the platform into their bases and up through their bodies in harmony with each other.

Starlah could feel both their hearts beating in unison. Her perineum tingled with the burst of electrified currents seeping from his body into hers through the quartz's platform. It swirled through her pelvis, causing her to gasp and squirm. She no longer had it in her to hold his gaze and closed her eyes, allowing waves of energy to trickle up her spine, igniting each part of her body with delicious, exhilarating ripples of energy.

Both their pendants hummed in unison against their chests, and when the resonance reached a certain peak the two crystal pendants gravitated towards each other. The ripples of discharged energy from both crystals let off crackling. The pull towards each crystal was so intense and palpable; finally they touched and locked into each other to form a single flame.

A final ecstatic surge of energy burst through Starlah and Ardaleigh's bodies as their pendants locked into place. Starlah moaned, and they both collapsed into each other, heaving and elated.

They laid in each other's arms, completely satiated and content being in the moment, not allowing the knowledge that Starlah would be sent back to cloud their joy. 'Ardaleigh …'

'Mm, yes my love?'

'I know it's such a Third Realm thing to say, but—I love you.'

Ardaleigh smiled and kissed the top of her head. 'I like that saying very much, and I love you too.' He leaned in and kissed her lips.

'Good. Just as well or there would be …' She stopped and frowned. 'It seems I must go now. Eldest Brother has summoned my return.' She sighed, held him and kissed him with conviction before she was returned to the Third Realm.

TWELVE

STARLAH LAY on her bed, unwilling to relinquish the connection to Ardaleigh. She breathed deeply and focused her mind on his gentle embrace, his smile and his love for her. If she squeezed her eyes tight enough and blocked out everything else she could deceive her senses and believe he was still next to her.

Eventually the Third Realm filtered through. The light traffic noise outside the window polluted her ears, the pressure of the crumbled doona beneath her irritated her back and the loneliness played *ha-ha* games with her heart.

She tried to soothe the tumultuous throb in her chest by placing her hand over her heart, hoping it was a worthy enough gesture to appease its ache and bear the acceptance that the precious moments with Ardaleigh would have to exist on the outskirts of her consciousness.

She refused reality's intrusion. She hoped that by keeping her eyes closed she could avoid the story it wanted her to rejoice in. Its cruelty seemed unnecessary. The endless cycle of rebirth left her feeling punished and exiled. But she couldn't remember why. What was it that she had to transcend before it was too late? She squeezed her eyes and searched her brain. *Empty*—guess her mother was right after all.

The turbulence in her mind was driving her to the fine line of insanity. Would ignorance be a saner option for her? She was sure that if she beseeched the Eldest Brother he would erase her awareness of both worlds. But then she wouldn't remember Ardaleigh and all that he meant to her. She knew she would just feel that something significant was missing but be oblivious to what that emptiness represented.

Delusion no longer wanted to play her game; it compelled her to open her eyes and forced her life back in. A pain so deep and harrowing rippled through her momentarily, she gasped with the intensity. It was a reminder of her ability to love, despite it all. Without that reminder he would disappear from her consciousness, and she would be lost again.

She gritted her teeth and forced her body to resume living. She would do everything in her power to solve the riddle that was her life. She would do anything to get back to Ardaleigh.

Darting her eyes around the room, accepting this reality fully however startled her as to how easily the memory of his touch, his taste, his voice dimmed with each passing second until she could be forgiven for doubting his very existence. This time she would not let go of his memory. She would hold onto her love so he would remain real—always.

She looked down at herself and felt the loss of her Fourth Realm body. Over the past three years she had come to accept her Third Realm body but even though it was well toned and attractive, something had been missing. Maybe she only knew her beauty through the arms and eyes of Ardaleigh.

She heard the front door being opened and Daniel talking on his phone as he walked in. *Thank God,* she thought, *a distraction.* She tiptoed to the door and strained to hear. He was yelling at someone on the other end.

'I told you a month ago, I don't want anything to do with that shit no more. Seriously I'm done. You can tell Davo I'm done— OK.' He walked through the apartment, and Starlah could hear him head into his room.

Starlah forced herself to leave her room, lest it became her crypt and walked out to the living room and retreated to the sofa, waiting for him to finish. She needed to feel grounded in this reality, and Danny always made her feel loved. She could use that to keep her from falling to pieces.

After five minutes he stormed out of his room, mumbling. He stopped when he saw her. 'Shit Starlah, I didn't think you were home. What the hell are you doing, creeping around like that?' He glowered.

She tilted her head. 'OK then. A little agro, are we?'

He rubbed his head and looked around the room.

What the hell is he looking so guilty about? she wondered. But given his agro meter had been amped to blast mode she didn't dare ask him.

'Sorry—um, just scared me. That's all.' He walked into the kitchen and opened the fridge. She heard him mumble something as he grabbed a bottle of beer.

'What was that?' she asked, thinking he was talking to her.

'Seriously, do you gotta know everything?' he barked as he unscrewed the top to the beer and took a big gulp.

Starlah cringed. He'd never gone off at her before and she didn't know how to handle him when he was so edgy. Her desperate need to feel connected and loved was evaporating.

'Sorry,' she said, studying him. She couldn't help but notice the Rose gene coming out in him more and more lately. She looked away and decided to go back to her room and allow him time to chill. No doubt, after a few beers he would settle, she thought bitterly.

Even though Daniel had been away from their parents for the past ten years they still lingered on the outskirts of his personality. Some of Daddy's quirks had been passed on to him—nothing too serious, just a few mannerism and habits like his drinking and rubbing his head whenever he felt agitated. But it was enough to trigger a physical response in Starlah.

The more he remained elusive, the more she felt distant from him, and a faint corner of her heart trembled with the fear of being abandoned yet again. She couldn't bear losing Daniel again so if that meant she had to let him have his secrets, then that was what she needed to do, for now anyway.

She knew that sooner or later she wouldn't be able to hold off delving into his mystery. She hoped he wouldn't hate her when she succumbed to her detective impulses.

There was a gentle tap on her door. 'Hey Starbright, can I come in?' Daniel stuck his head through the door, grinning in an exaggerated manner. He looked totally goofy.

Starlah laughed. 'Who can say no to a face like that?'

Danny walked in, sat on her bed and sighed. 'Starbright, you're the last person I want to get shitty with. It's just that my past won't leave me alone.' He stared down at his hands.

She noticed the scars across his knuckles and wished she could ask him how he had gotten them. 'It's OK Danny; you don't have to tell me.' She looked away and braced herself.

He put his hand on her shoulder. 'It's all good, nothing I can't handle, really.' He hesitated.

She waited for him to continue. He opened and closed his mouth a few times trying to form words, but none seemed to be forthcoming.

Starlah's heart raced. If it was so hard for him to utter the words how bad was it? She rubbed her neck; she didn't want to know just yet. 'Hey …' She jumped up off the bed. 'I met up with Jasmine, and I told her what happened.' She paced around the room, distracting him from what he wanted to tell her.

'Oh, how'd that go?' He followed her with his eyes.

'Um, pretty bad actually.' She stopped and stared at herself in the mirror, avoiding his concerned eyes. She didn't want to lose it again. Dark halos accentuated her eyes, making her look raccoon-y. She shrugged, supposing that in some parts of the world that would be considered a sexy look. It didn't seem to be working for her though.

She had to look away. Her own face wasn't making her feel

any more in control of her emotions. Tears played pull ups on her lower eyelids, seeking victory over the rim. She blinked, shoving them back down.

'Yeah, what did she say?'

'Well, Jaz was good and it was a relief to tell her, but Bella turned up and went off at me.' She cringed and shook her head. 'She doesn't believe me, and now she hates me.' She looked over at Daniel.

He stood up, walked over to her and hugged her against his chest. 'I'm proud of you. That must've been so hard to do. Give her time. It's not easy having to face that kind of truth about someone you love.' He kissed her on the side of her head. 'Bet she'll come 'round.'

'Yeah, I don't know about that. She was pretty guttered.' She closed her eyes and hugged Daniel, drawing strength from him, hoping she finally had control over her weepy eyelids.

He pushed her out and looked down at her. 'How about you and I get dressed up and go out for dinner tonight? Sara's working so it's just the two of us. Somewhere fancy, my shout.' He waited for her to respond.

She fake-smiled. 'Sure, love to.'

'Cool. A friend of my works up in Brisbane at this five-star hotel. Bet he could get us a table at the seafood buffet there. What do you reckon?'

Starlah nodded. 'Sounds great.' Sometimes it was easier to allow the distraction than to dig too deep when it came to Daniel. Besides, a nice dinner out would be a welcome relief from her ordinary cooking attempts and her heartache at being away from Ardaleigh.

THIRTEEN

STARLAH REACHED over and fiddled with the radio until she came across a song she liked. She cranked up the volume, allowing the music to settle her nerves. Daniel had remained quiet since they had gotten into the car so she needed the music as a distraction.

She stared at his profile while he focused on the road. Every few minutes, he would chew on the corner of his bottom lip as though he was deliberating. What the hell had he gotten himself into?

The roads were fairly clear, and they pulled up to the hotel right on time. They walked through the foyer and were greeted by a pretty young girl in a floral uniform.

Behind her approached a burly guy. 'Oh hey, it's Danny boy.' He smiled as he walked around the counter and came to greet them. 'I've got this one, Paige.' He dismissed her.

'OK boss.' Paige smiled at Starlah and Daniel and went back to her duties.

'So freaking great to see ya.' He slapped Daniel on the back. 'Let me show you guys to the table.' He guided them around a few tables until he came to a table for two right next to the buffet.

Starlah glanced at the food, but she must have left her appetite back home. Nothing tempted her, despite looking and smelling amazing.

'This is Dave, a friend of mine,' Daniel finally introduced them. 'Dave, this is my kid sister, Starlah.'

'Hey, nice to meet ya. You didn't tell me you had a hot kid sister, Danny boy.' Dave leaned over and shook Starlah's hand.

She didn't want to seem rude and smiled. 'Yeah, you too Dave.' She eyed him, trying to suss out what role he played in Daniel's life.

Daniel darted his eyes at Starlah then Dave. 'Easy there, *bro*, don't want to have to break your leg.' His mouth smiled, but his eyes relayed a warning.

Dave lifted his hands in the air. 'Righto, no need for that, Danny boy. Just kidding.' He laughed and pulled out the chair for Starlah to have a seat. She sat, and he pushed the chair in for her.

Daniel seated himself and smiled stiffly. 'Thanks, Dave. This is great.'

Dave smiled in return. 'No probs, bro. Enjoy.' He left them at their table and went back to his duties. Daniel stared at his friend as he retreated, the corner of his mouth twitching.

Starlah peered at Daniel. He noticed and smiled. 'How good is this, hey?' He looked around the beautifully decorated room. The restaurant was decked out with immaculate tables with white linen tablecloths, sparkling cutlery and crisp white plates. The centre of the room was loaded with all sorts of seafood, salads, cold cuts and various other hot and cold foods.

'Hope you're hungry.' Daniel nodded at all the food.

'You bet.' Her stomach contracted into a nervous tight knot. Although she didn't know what was going on with Daniel she knew something wasn't right. She darted her eyes towards Dave. He was busy talking with some other staff members. He must have sensed her staring at him. He looked over, grinned and waved. She smiled back.

'I'll go get us some drinks; you can go help yourself to the grub.' Daniel jumped out of the chair and headed towards the bar.

Dave saw him approaching and met him at the bar. The two of them stepped to the side and got into what looked like a heated discussion.

At one point Starlah was about to jump up and run to Daniel's aid, but he looked over, smiled and waved his hand for her to go get something to eat. She reluctantly got to her feet and made her way to the buffet. She mindlessly piled on prawns, crab meat and several scoops of salad and then drizzled some vinaigrette dressing all over the plate.

On her way back to the table she went the long way around the back so she had to pass the bar. As she approached she saw Dave shove a finger at Daniel's chest. 'You still owe us, bro—'

Daniel saw Starlah approaching and started to laugh. 'Righto

Dave, see what I can do about that.' With that he walked over to Starlah. 'Hey, that looks great. 'Bout time I got me some.' He put his hand briefly onto Starlah's shoulder as he walked past, heading towards the buffet table. She'd swear she felt his hand tremble.

Starlah moved the food around the plate. The prawns' beady eyes stared at her. *What the hell are you looking at?* She glared back at them. She moved a lettuce leaf so it covered them. *There now, stare through that.*

Silence sat between them as though it was an invisible boulder. Every few seconds she would look up and stare at Daniel. What was he thinking? He seemed completely lost. But when he broke from his own moving-around food activity and looked up at her she darted her eyes around the room as though she was interested in what was going on around her.

Starlah looked back down, moved the food on her plate again and accidentally unshielded the prawns. *Damn,* those beady eyes stared at her again. She gave up and dropped her fork. 'Danny, is everything OK?' she whispered.

'Mmm, what? Yeah sure, nothing to be stressing over.' He swallowed hard and stared out towards the corner of the room, where Dave was talking on the phone. 'Don't be worrying about Davo. He's pissed at me for messing up his plans, that's all. Nothing I can't handle.'

Starlah stared over at Dave as well and scrunched her eyes,

trying to extract some sort of vibe from him. He looked elegant and authoritarian in his black suit, but there was something about the way he held his body and his attempts at hiding his tattoos around the top of his chest that reminded her of one of the guys from *Sons of Anarchy*. She looked at Danny's arms and studied the tattoos peering out from under his T-shirt. She wondered if they had gotten them at the same place.

'Are you in some sort of trouble?' She stared into his eyes. He looked tired and sad.

'I hope not.' He looked down at his half-eaten meal and sighed. 'I really thought all that crap from my lock-up days was done with, but'—he looked over towards Dave again and sighed—'it seems that I've still got debt to pay.'

She opened her mouth to say something, but it got stuck.

'I don't want you to be stressing over any of this, OK?' He reached out and placed his hand onto Starlah's.

She looked down at his hand and studied the scars across his knuckles again. She tried not to freak out and took a deep breath. She desperately wanted to know what the hell he had gotten himself into, but a small part of her still begged for ignorance, the same part that convinced her heart when growing up that the abuse her parents dished out wasn't so bad.

Out of the corner of her eye Starlah saw Dave approaching, carrying a black folder with their bill in it. He advanced, smiling, with his chin in the air. 'Hey, how'd you enjoy your dinner, guys?' He stood at the table and looked into Starlah's eyes.

'Yeah, it was great, thanks,' she answered as she looked away. His dark brown eyes felt too invasive.

'Sweet. Well, here's your bill. I've given you guys the mate's rate.' He grinned as he passed the folder over to Daniel.

Daniel picked up the folder and opened it. He seized a card, read it and shoved it into his pocket. He then pulled out his credit card, put it into the folder and handed it back to Dave. 'Thanks Dave, dinner was great, and it was great to see you.' He tried to smile convincingly.

Dave laughed, picked up the folder and slapped Danny on the back. 'No probs, bro. Anything for a mate.' He walked off, whistling.

Starlah's nerves were playing havoc with her stomach: either that or Davo was trying to poison them with a heavy dose of laxatives. Her belly quivered as she jumped to her feet. 'Be back in a minute.'

Daniel looked up at her and frowned. 'Where you going?'

There was no time for explanations. She took off in a hurry and burst through the door. Just as well no one was in the toilet—or they would have been privy to some pretty impressive sound effects.

She shoved open the toilet door; it whacked against the wall. She eyed off the seat but didn't have time to wipe it down or cover it with toilet paper as she normally would have. She sat down and let go of the day's tension rippling through her stomach.

She heard someone walk in. She remained quiet, but they left in a hurry. Finally the cramps stopped, and she swiftly finished up and pretty much ran to the basin, hoping to leave before anyone walked in and discovered who was responsible for the aroma.

She washed her hands, avoiding eye contact with the geisha staring through the mirror at her. She frowned, sure that shade of white sort of suited her, but if she was going to go full geisha, she would need to add some red to her lips.

She turned the tap off, flicked the water off her hands and took a deep breath—well, as deep as she dared, given the state of the surrounding air. She finally came to a resolution; if she didn't want constant stomach issues, she needed to let Danny be his own man. She needed to stop worrying about him and his decisions.

OK? She nodded at the geisha. The geisha confirmed and nodded back. Right, so just breathe and let him be. She exhaled and wiped her hands on a paper towel. By the time she was ready to step out of the toilets she was a fraction calmer and in control of her bodily functions.

She swung open the door and stepped out of the toilet, oblivious to her surroundings, not wanting to maintain eye contact with anyone in case they were heading in after her. She bumped into someone coming out of the men's toilets. 'Oh, sorry.' She looked up and froze. Her heart stopped for a second, registered that it was Brad and then broke into a high tempo.

'Well, lookie what we have here. So nice to see you, Starlah.' He smirked.

She stumbled and backed herself into the wall. She had a flashback to that night. Her legs quivered.

He stepped forward, staring into her eyes. 'Been a while, hey? So how's things?'

Her hand automatically clutched her pendant; it burned. She

could feel Ardaleigh close by. She remembered her sovereign's words and yelled in her mind, *'No, don't. I can handle this. Stay out of it.'*

The pendant cooled as she felt him stepping back. She exhaled in relief. She couldn't bear him being punished for her. She refocused her attention to the problem in front of her. She dragged a deep breath in, pulling her shoulders back and shoved him hard.

He went flying backwards into the wall. He laughed. 'Well, look who's all feisty.' He stepped forward. 'I love that.'

She glared at him. Her hands were bunched up into tight balls. Fury burned through her. This time, she was going to punch, scratch, kick—anything to make him hurt back.

He stepped forward and smirked, and he raised his hand as though he wanted to caress her face. She raised her knee, getting ready. But just as his hand was about to connect with her skin he went flying backwards.

At first Starlah thought Ardaleigh had broken his promise, but then she realised it was Daniel who had ripped Brad off her. Daniel swung Brad around and threw a punch into his face. Brad's head jerked to the side and blood splattered from his nose.

He grabbed his nose, yelling, 'You fuckin' broke my nose, you arsehole.' Blood seeped through his fingers and dribbled onto the floor.

Daniel's face was blazing red as he pulled back his arm, readying himself to land more punches into Brad.

Starlah yelled, 'Stop, Danny, he's not worth it. Please.'

Dave raced around the corner, grabbed Daniel around the

neck and pulled him off Brad. He held him while he thrashed, trying to pull free. 'Not here, not now. Do your job, and it will be paid forward. Got it?'

Daniel's face contorted in rage, and his chest heaved with deep breaths. But he allowed himself to be pulled away from Brad. Starlah now understood how he got all those scars across his knuckles. Blood oozed from them. She clutched herself, shaking.

Dave let Daniel go, stepped forward, grabbed Brad around his upper arm and shoved a napkin into his face. 'Get the hell outta here, or I will let him loose on you.' He shoved Brad hard, and Brad stumbled forward.

Brad turned and glared at them all. 'Be seeing ya, Starlah.' He winked at her as he mopped the blood from his face. He turned and then ran out.

She gritted her teeth. She so wanted to scratch his eyeballs out. She'd like to see him try to wink at her with no eyes. So many feelings and emotions swirled through her. Fear sat beside rage, which strangely felt empowering. Living with the type of parents she had never allowed her to develop any sense of empowerment. All she ever knew was fear and subservience, but a new strength filled her demanding respect. She wasn't going to let Brad take that from her.

She turned and looked at Daniel. His chest was still heaving and his fists were clenched. If she had allowed it she was sure that he would have done some serious life-threatening harm to Brad. For a split second she allowed herself to entertain that possibility. *No, not worth it,* she told herself.

She went over to Daniel and wrapped her arms around him.

She could feel him calming down. 'Thank you, Danny. Thanks for being there when I need you the most.' She kissed him on the cheek.

'Always Sis, always.' He hugged her tightly, shaking with the effects from the adrenaline pumping through him.

She clutched her pendant. It remained cool, but she knew there were two men who would do anything to protect her. She felt her eyes water. She loved them both.

'Righto, that was intense, hey.' Dave laughed. 'Danny boy's got himself a bit of a temper—liking that,' he joked.

Starlah glared at him and grabbed Daniel by the arm. 'Come on, let's get out of here.' She dragged him towards the door.

Daniel allowed her to walk him out. He turned once they reached the front door and stared at Dave.

'Be seeing you, Danny boy. Don't forget what you gotta do. Do it, and that problem with the little dweeb will be sorted for you.' He waved as they walked out the door and into the cool night.

FOURTEEN

STARLAH SAT in the car with her arms wrapped around herself. Even though the night air was cool it was still pleasant, yet she couldn't shake the chill running through her. The ride back home was more awkward than getting there. This time she allowed the silence, preferring to keep the music off.

She concentrated on Daniel's breathing, waiting for it to slow. After a while he took a deep breath and blew out hard. She sighed in return.

He turned and looked at her. 'You OK?'

She tried to smile, but it only came out across half of her face. 'Yeah, I'm OK. I was dreading running into him, but strangely I wasn't too freaked out.' She turned away and looked out the window. 'Huh, must have been all those counselling sessions,' she concluded as she chewed on her nails.

Even though she wasn't a crumbling mess on the floor she still didn't want to have to face him again. But his face taunted her. The way he winked at her and said he'd be seeing her made her shiver. Was that only a threat, or did he mean it?

She allowed Dave's words to soothe her: '… that problem with the little dweeb will be sorted …' What exactly did that mean, and what did Daniel have to do for it to be sorted?

She winced as she bit into flesh, realising that she had chewed off all her nails. She sucked on her throbbing finger. Aargh! Why did life have to be so freaking hard? Seriously, why couldn't she plod along, being happy with an ordinary existence, never facing anything more challenging than what TV program to watch?

She thought back to a few hours ago and how she was lying in Ardaleigh's arms in the Chamber of Resonance, completely content and in love. She closed her eyes, pictured his soothing caresses and wanted to cry. Why couldn't she be back there? What had she done to have made the Bludlin Guild send her to this life? And what soul truth did she have to uncover and transcend?

For a split second an image flashed through her mind, an image of her standing over a bloodied figure holding a stone dripping with blood. She snapped open her eyes and sucked in a breath, clutching her throat.

'What?' Daniel looked at her with concern.

She darted her eyes around the car and then looked at Daniel. She had no idea if the image was real, but it caused her body to respond as though it was. 'Nothing—stomach's still unsettled.' She leaned forward and clutched her stomach. She didn't dare close her eyes again.

He looked at her briefly, and then back at the road. 'OK, we'll be home in ten minutes.' He frowned. 'Can you hold on?'

She sat back and took a deep breath. 'Yeah, I'll be fine.' She rubbed her stomach and visualised the toilet scene back at the restaurant. She shook; she certainly didn't want any more explosive episodes like that, especially while she was in Daniel's car.

FIFTEEN

STARLAH LAY on her bed and stared up at the ceiling, the lamp casting ghoulish shadows throughout her room. She concentrated on the outline of the shadows and tried to make out faces, like she used to do when she was younger. But only rock-shaped images danced around, taunting her.

Every time she closed her eyes the bloodied rock raced towards her face. Every time she would snap open her eyes and grip her sheets, waiting for the impact. She begged for sleep, but was afraid what images might invade her dreams so she concentrated on keeping her eyelids wide open. By 2 am they each weighed about twenty kilos and insisted on closing. She gave in and drifted off into Slumber Land.

Slumber Land beckoned her forth. *'Come, enter, see what wonders lay beyond ...'* She tentatively entered through the wooden gates and walked across the pebbled pathway through to the cosy cottage, surrounded by lush greenery and beautiful multi-coloured flowers.

She stood at the pale, weathered wooden door, raised her hand and then stopped. She turned her head and looked around the scenery, wondering where she was. Somehow it felt familiar.

She looked down at herself and saw a small-framed pale figure dressed in a sky-blue thin bliaut with a golden woven belt tied around her petite waist. She raised her hand and caressed her thick dark-plaited hair, which flowed down to her waist.

'Saimira, is that you hath come home?' a voice called behind the door.

Starlah spun her head around and found her mouth answering, 'Yea Moder, 'tis I, returned from the market.' She opened the door and walked into the dimly lit, sparse room as though she had done it a million times before.

'Arg child, look at you. You resemble a forgotten child, with no loving kin to keep you kempt.' Her mother walked over and fussed with her face, wiping dirt off her cheeks.

'Nay need fussing, nay suitors were met along the way.' Saimira giggled.

'Hush, your fader take to your behind if he hear you gibber like that.' He mother smiled at her and flicked her with the handtowel, then walked into the small kitchen and fiddled with the dough she had rolled out. 'Do not forget your childhad is behind you. You are a young lady, and you must learn to behave as such.'

'Yea, Moder.' She smiled at her mother fondly.

Saimira heard her father and brother coming up the pathway, talking loudly as they approached.

'Quick Saimira, set the table ready for your fader's ale.' Her mother fussed, getting ready to pour her father his welcome home drink.

Saimira did as she was told and grabbed two large mugs so her father and Jacob could relax after their hard day out in the fields.

'Good day, women folk.' Her father stomped his feet at the door, removing the dirt that clung to his boots.

'Good day, Fader and Jacob,' her mother called in a joyful voice. She walked over to greet them. 'How was your day?' She lovingly placed her hand over her husband's heart and looked into his eyes, her daily ritual upon his return.

He placed his rough, calloused hand onto her shoulder and squeezed affectionately. 'An honest day's done, dear.' He smiled at her and then looked at Saimira, 'Young Saimira, how was your day occupied?'

'Mindfully, Fader,' she answered as she walked towards him and gave him a hug.

He squeezed her gently and smiled, 'As a young lady should.' He went and sat down at the small wooden table with only two chairs that were shared amongst them. The women waited on the men and would eat after the men were finished. 'Ah, I am hunger bitten and could eat the hind of a hart.'

'Pour us a drink,' Jacob ordered Saimira as he took the other seat. He looked at Saimira with a stern expression. Even though Jacob was only three years older than she, at sixteen he took it upon himself to be her master.

She gritted her teeth and did as she was told. She raised the decanter and poured them their frothing ales. 'Here, Jacob.' She placed his drink down with a thud, spilling some of it. She placed her father's down gently and smiled into his green eyes.

'Thanks, Dother.' Her father picked up his mug and slurped on his ale.

Saimira stared at Jacob, wanting to spill the ale over his head. He had been bothersome these past few weeks, following her around, spying on her and being fatherly. She had a father and didn't want another. But something had changed between them. Ever since her bleeding had arrived marking her womanhood, he seemed overly observant. Who does Jacob think he is? Well, certainly not her minder, she avowed.

Saimira huffed to herself and helped her mother prepare their evening meal while running scenarios of what she would do the next time she found Jacob spying.

Starlah awoke with the buzzing of the alarm ringing in her ear. The image of her dream lingered through her mind. She ran her hand over her head to make sure that she was herself and not stuck in time as her Saimira self.

Was that what that was, a look at herself from the past? It was hard to tell what was going on these days, with her being teleported back and forth between realms. Seriously, if she confessed these things to her counsellor she'd probably be locked up for delusions. Yet the truth remained the truth. Now the task was how to handle that truth.

YOUNGER BROTHER Ardaleigh, I am going to strongly reaffirm the need for you to be re-born in the Third Realm. I feel you'll benefit from another life there.' Tomace stared into Ardaleigh's eyes and welcomed a challenge.

He squinted and studied Ardaleigh's expression. When he couldn't extract the response he desired, he continued. 'Your obsession with Starlah is contaminating all our minds.' He turned and looked out towards the courtyard, where Katalin was watering a row of ulander flowers. He ran his hand over his pendant and smiled.

'You see, not all of us feel the need to act as love-struck fools when it comes to our twin flame.' He spun around and refocused his attention onto Ardaleigh. 'At our next meeting I am going to petition the Harper Guild. I can be quite persuasive, Younger Brother.' He smirked.

Ardaleigh remained quiet and simply stared at Tomace. He tried to remember how the two of them were ever friends. Tomace possessed a need for dominance; however, as one evolved and ascended the needs of the ego were supposed to be left behind. Yet Ardaleigh had a feeling that Tomace was struggling with this notion.

Ardaleigh smiled and stepped forward so he was right in front of Tomace and the two of them were eye to eye. 'Brother Tomace, as easy as it is for the Harper Guild to consent to my rebirth it is just as easy to consent to yours. I may be struggling with Starlah's rebirth, but I have a strong feeling your own struggle with your ego's need for dominance may warrant another life through the Third Realm also.'

He turned, looked out towards the courtyard and nodded in the direction of Katalin. 'I'm sure that you will gain a better understanding of the pain I feel when one of the two of you is sent on a rebirth journey for the betterment of your development. You see, Brother, I too can be persuasive. If I petition the Guild, particularly Katalin, and appeal that yours or her rebirth would help resolve your ego needs I'm sure they would see the benefit of such a request.' He turned and smiled back at Tomace.

Tomace's smirk faded as the truth of Ardaleigh's words registered. He swallowed hard. 'Well Brother, I see your point, but don't think that I wouldn't sacrifice myself or Katalin to ensure you get the necessary life experiences to help *you* evolve.'

Ardaleigh bowed his head. 'As you wish, Elder Brother. I guess the both of us have requests to share at the next meeting.'

He kept his head lowered and exited the chambers. He walked past Katalin and smiled at her.

She smiled in return. 'Greetings, Younger Brother. Is everything all right between you and Tomace?' She looked concerned, darting her eyes from Ardaleigh to Tomace, who was standing in the doorway.

'Everything is wonderful, Elder Sister, just a catch-up with a past friend.' Ardaleigh looked back at Tomace and nodded. 'Isn't that right, Elder Brother?'

Tomace forced a smile. 'Indeed, always a pleasure to catch up with an old friend.' He lingered a moment at the door and then turned and headed back into his white domed-shaped chambers, leaving Katalin staring suspiciously at Ardaleigh.

'What was that about?' She lowered the watering canister and stepped forward so she was in front of Ardaleigh and looked into his eyes.

Ardaleigh found it impossible to keep things from her when she stared at him like that. Lying was not a trait common in the Fourth Realm as most people could read the energy of a lie. But sometimes holding back the truth was accepted, except when Katalin's eyes looked imploringly into his own. He held genuine warmth and affection for his Elder Sister and hated having conflict with her twin flame.

'It seems Brother Tomace feels strongly about my rebirth. I hope that his opinion isn't supported by all members of the Elders.' Ardaleigh dropped his eyes and looked down at the cut flower in her hand. He couldn't bear seeing her eyes betray her when she denied that she felt that way also.

'Brother Ardaleigh, sometimes we cannot see the benefit of such a journey until the journey has been completed. I know better than most the heartache you feel at the absence of Starlah.' She reached her hand out and gently grabbed his. 'But I know how important it is that she complete this cycle.'

Ardaleigh looked back up into Katalin's eyes and sighed. 'I know, Sister. I know.' He looked out towards the horizon and took a deep breath. 'Knowing that still doesn't take away the pain and longing. The idea of being forced to spend another cycle without her …' He closed his eyes and fought back tears. 'I don't think I could endure that.'

'Ardaleigh, I will support you with whatever you deem apt for your advancement. If you accept your feelings, spend time in the reflection chamber and learn to integrate these emotions and desires, then channel them more beneficially, I will vote against rebirth.'

Ardaleigh squeezed her hand. 'Thank you, Sister, that's all I can ask of you. The rest is up to the other six members. Well, five as I already know how Tomace feels.' He walked away, clutching his pendant and praying that at the next meeting he still found himself grounded in the Fourth Realm.

SEVENTEEN

STARLAH HESITANTLY got out of bed and headed into the kitchen. After the weirdness of last night's events with Davo, Brad and the Saimira dream she didn't know what this day would bring. She was relieved when she didn't find Daniel in the kitchen. She needed some time to think about everything.

She saw the jacket Daniel wore last night and remembered the card he slipped into one of the pockets. She walked over to it and stared at it, assessing the danger. She waited a few moments to see if the sleeves would leap up and slap her in the face yelling, 'What the hell do you think you're doing?' When no slapping action commenced she walked past the jacket and ran her hand over the side panel, just casually. There was no need to look suspicious.

When her hand traced over the pocket she felt the edges of

the card. She tried to absorb its contents through the material but soon discovered she lack the ability to absorb information via osmosis into her hands. *Damn,* she would have to delve into the pocket and pull out the card.

Her heart tripped over a few times as she stuck her hand into the pocket and pulled out the card that Davo snuck to Daniel after dinner. It looked harmless enough; it was a business card from the hotel with Davo's contacts on it, as the hotel manager. Huh, not much of a secret revelation there. She flipped it over and discovered a message.

7552 RED DIAMOND

CASUALITY MEMBER – DADDIO

REACTIVATE MEMBERSHIP 48/24

Hm OK, that was a bit more of a secret revelation, but it made no sense. She heard Daniel stirring in his room, so she fumbled putting the card back. She smoothed over the wrinkles in his jacket and sat down on the sofa, looking all innocent-like. Her heart's erratic beating was the only sign of her betrayal.

He stumbled out of the room, coughing, clearing his throat. 'Morning, did you manage to sleep OK?' He rubbed his hand over his head a few times and headed into the kitchen, straight for the fridge. He opened it, pulled out the orange juice, flipped off the lid and drank straight from the bottle, sculling what remained in the bottle in one mouthful. 'Ah, that's better.' He burped, wiped his hand across his mouth and then looked at Starlah, waiting for a response.

She darted her eyes from his jacket to him and answered hurriedly, 'Yeah sure. Fine, I'm all fine–um–why–yeah good, thanks.' She grimaced and looked away.

He chuckled and tilted his head. 'Um OK, what are you tripping on?' He put the empty bottle of juice back into the fridge; well technically there was about two millimetres left. He sat down beside her and smiled into her face. 'So what are you hiding? I know you, Starbright, you're up to something.'

She laughed, though it came out as though she was Santa doing her best 'HO, HO, HO' interpretation. 'Oh Danny, you're funny–nothing–um–I'm not hiding anything. What? No idea what you're talking about. ' She jumped up to her feet and headed into the kitchen. 'So can I make you some brekky?' She exhaled, dropping her shoulders from around her ears.

He laughed and shook his head. 'Yeah, whatever you say, Starbright. Sure, scrambled eggs sounds perfect, thanks.' He got to his feet and headed back to his room. 'Just gonna have a quick shower; be back by the time brekky's ready.' He grinned at her and closed the door to his room.

She slumped onto the counter and softly banged her head, repeating, *So stupid, stupid*, under her breath. She straightened herself, flicked her hands down her front and inhaled her crazy. *Right, get it together. Breakfast ain't gonna make itself.*

She finished making the scrambled eggs and placed them clumsily across the plate next to a piece of burnt toast. She picked the plate for herself where the toast looked most burnt and placed the plates on top of the breakfast bench, waiting for Daniel to come back out.

He raced out of his room, dressed in a pair of dark denim jeans and a pale blue T-shirt. 'Smells amazing.' He plonked himself onto the stool and grabbed his fork, getting ready to down the first mouthful. He spotted the burnt toast, hesitated but then continued to scoop up the egg. He looked up at Starlah and smiled widely, showing off bits of egg in his mouth. 'Delicious. Thanks.'

She smiled. He was adorable; he'd never dream of hurting her by complaining about the failed effort. That's why she would do whatever she could to protect him.

'So what are you up to today?' She picked up her own fork and scooped up some egg at least that looked safe enough to eat. She expected him to answer the usual: work with Jacko at the construction site.

'Think I'll just catch up with Sara for lunch. How about you?' He avoided eye contact as he scooped the remaining egg off his plate.

Why was he having lunch with his girlfriend and not going to work today? She looked down at her own plate. 'Yeah, probably hang out here and watch some DVDs.' She'd lied; she had other plans that involved her getting savvy on spy protocol.

'Cool …' He looked down at his plate and stared at the toast. 'Boy, I am full, couldn't possibly fit in another mouthful.' He wiped his mouth with a handtowel, picked up his plate and dropped the remaining food into the bin.

She smiled. 'I know right. Those eggs hit the spot, hey, don't reckon I'm gonna be able to fit the toast in either.' They both looked at each other and burst out laughing. 'You're such a liar, Danny. I know how crap the toast looks.'

He continued to chuckle, walked over to her and kissed the top of her head. 'Yeah, but I'd never say so.'

'That's why I love my big brother, knows when to lie. Hey?' She looked up into his face.

He looked away. 'Yeah sure. Sometimes a little lie is what's needed.' He pulled away and headed back to his room to finish getting ready. When he came back out a few minutes later he went over and grabbed his jacket. He put his hand into his pocket, mumbling, 'Now, where's my wallet?' When he felt the pocket with the card in it he said, 'Ah, there it is.'

Starlah's heart pounded. She knew he was lying. He was heading to wherever Davo wanted. The message on the card was the key.

'Right, see ya later, Starbright. Have fun watching those DVDs.' He grabbed his keys and headed out the door.

Starlah's instincts wanted her to follow him, but she was still in her PJs and her hair was flailing around her head like Medusa's snakes. She had to settle for some spy Google searching. Starting with what the hell '7552 Red Diamond' meant.

Starlah sat down in front of the laptop and typed in the search engine '7552 Red Diamond'. Nothing for '7552' came up. There were however references to red diamonds. Actual rare red diamonds. Could it literally have something to do with red diamonds? These were currently being showcased around the world and would be making the rounds through Perth, Sydney, New York, Tokyo and then Hong Kong.

Starlah jotted down the references and circled 'Red Diamond' at the top of the page with a big question mark next to the words 'actual diamonds'. She couldn't see Daniel having anything to do with diamonds, and the idea of him being involved in trying to steal those very rare expensive, as in multiple millions worth, diamonds—she just couldn't see it. The security involved would be far too sophisticated and dangerous. So perhaps the red diamond code stood for something else.

She clicked on an article referencing 'red diamond' as being the new street name for a synthetic drug making its rounds in American schools. There wasn't any mention of the drugs being on Australian streets yet, but what if it was here and the cops didn't know about it? She shivered. Nah, he wouldn't be so stupid surely.

She moved onto the second line: casualty member – Daddio. Hm, obviously 'casualty member' had something to do with Daddio being taken out somehow. So who was Daddio? And what did Daniel have to do to Daddio exactly? Her heart quickened. Surely that didn't mean anything permanent.

She heard his words in her head, 'I beat that poor man to an inch of his life …'

Was Daniel capable of 'taking out' the target? She would never believe that. The Daniel she knew, the one who comforted and protected her couldn't possibly be capable of doing that to someone. But then again Bella couldn't see her brother as a monster either.

She shook her head—no, not possible. He said that he was a different person now, and she believed him. But the question lingered: what was going to happen to Daddio?

She remembered the last line: 'reactivate membership 48/24'. Whose membership had to be reactivated and to what? What did '48/24' mean? She typed in '48/24' on the computer, and multiple references of time came up. 48/24 could indicate 48 hours. So that would mean that in 48 hours someone's, maybe Daniel's, membership had to be reactivated, but to what?

OK, so far she had references to actual red diamonds, maybe drugs. The target was Daddio, and possibly Daniel's membership to something had to be reactivated in 48 hours. She shook her head. She couldn't make any sense of how it explained Daniel's elusiveness.

EIGHTEEN

STARLAH RUBBED her eyes and then forcefully closed the laptop. *Useless gadget,* she insulted it before getting up and stretching her back and legs. She paced around the room running through the information she obtained, but she didn't have anything solid to go on. The few things she did have she refused to entertain as possibilities.

The word that kept jumping out at her was *drugs*. The next time he was heading out from home she would follow him. She would be ready. No Medusa hairdo or PJs would stop her. If she had to sleep standing in her clothes, then that's what she would do.

She needed to know what the hell he was involved in, no matter what the outcome. She shook her head. Her mind was all over the place. One minute she didn't want to know, and the next she had to know or she'd explode.

She walked into her room and sat down on her bed facing the mirror. She looked at herself and cringed. She looked tired and haggard, so much for not needing Botox yet—she shrugged to herself—whatever.

She picked up the brush and attempted to tame her wild flailing strands. As she battled with freeing the brush the weirdest thing happened; Saimira's face interposed hers and stared back at her in the mirror. Her heart jumped around erratically. She must be losing it.

'What do you want from me?' she yelled at herself in the mirror, with the brush still dangling from her hair.

Saimira's face tried to speak, but no sounds escaped the mirror. She looked torn and frightened. 'I am sorry,' she mouthed before fading back to Starlah. A sweat had broken out across her forehead. Maybe she should talk to her counsellor. Maybe she really was losing it.

She rubbed her eyes trying to get the image of Saimira's haunted face out of her mind. What was she sorry about? More importantly, what did this have to do with her life now? Her pendant heated up. She clutched it and took a deep breath: Ardaleigh? Tears stung her eyes. She so wished she was back in his arms.

She heard a whisper. 'Saimira has the answer to your return to me. Be brave, my love. Don't be afraid to look deeply at what was, so that what can be is made real once again.'

She closed her eyes and felt the lightest touch brush her cheek. She let tears wash down her face. She would do anything to be back in Ardaleigh's arms. If that meant she had to delve deeper into Saimira's life, well then, *Bring it, ghostly medieval girl. What deep dark secret do you feel the need to share with me?*

She shook her head and let out a nervous chuckle, must be going nuts for sure. Halfway through shaking her head the brush went flying and hit the mirror. She jumped and shivered. That's all she needed, seven more years of hell.

She got off the bed and turned away from the mirror. Even though she invited the truth now wasn't so good for her. Sorry. She hurried out of the room and stood in the lounge. She took a few deep breaths and tried to stop her hands from shaking.

'Must be the DTs,' she whispered, but remembered she didn't really drink. She rubbed her hands together and willed them to behave. 'It's OK, nothing to be freaking out over. Just might be going crazy—nothing to panic about.' She tried to calm herself down, but her pep talk wasn't doing much to actually calm her nerves.

Her mobile rang and she jumped. She spun her head in the direction of the ringing and crouched down in hunting mode. She couldn't remember where she left it and had to track it down before the ringing stopped. When she narrowed in on the target she pounced onto the couch, dug through the cushions and rescued her phone. Just as she went to swipe her finger across, unlocking the mystery caller's voice, it stopped ringing. 'Bugger,' she yelled.

She stared at her phone; the caller ID read 'unknown'. She waited to see if someone was leaving a message. After a few seconds the phone beeped, indicating that a message was left. She tapped in the numbers and listened to the mystery caller.

'Hi Starlah, thought I'd check in with you and let you know that I'm thinking of you.'

Her heart stopped. She would recognise his voice anywhere. *Brad.* She threw her phone back on to the couch and stared at it as if somehow he could squeeze out of the screen. She clutched herself and darted her eyes around the room. Her skin felt like spiders were crawling across her. 'What the fuck does he want?' she yelled at the phone.

You, it answered back. OK, so it didn't exactly answer back, but she knew what he wanted. She wasn't sure if that meant he was coming to get her or if he was just getting off on tormenting her.

Her phone rang again. She jumped and stared at it. She was too afraid to pick it up, so she leaned over and tried to read the ID. No, still an unknown number. 'Aargh, I ain't letting him freak me out.' She grabbed the phone and answered the call.

'Yeah, what the hell do you want, arsehole?' she yelled.

'Starlah, is that you?' a female voice responded.

'Um yeah, sorry, thought you were someone else.' Starlah cringed and rubbed her forehead. This day was not getting any better.

'Clearly. Is everything all right?' Sara's calm and welcoming voice soothed Starlah's nerves.

'Yeah, just thought you were the telemarketer annoying me again. Seriously, those guys just won't let up.' She tried to laugh it off.

'Oh, OK then, you know if you need to talk, I'm here for you.'

'Thanks Sara, but I'm fine … really I am. How can I help you?' She hoped that Sara would allow her to change the subject.

'Oh yeah, just hoping you know where Daniel is. I've tried ringing his phone heaps of times, and it keeps going to message bank. He was supposed to meet me for coffee before I leave to go to my mum's.' She cleared her throat and hesitated before continuing. 'Is everything OK with him? Has he said anything to you? It's just—I kinda get a feeling something's going on with him.' She echoed Starlah's concerns.

'Nah Sara, he's fine. I think the guys at work have been giving him a hard time, but it's nothing to do with you or how he feels about you.' She tried to sound upbeat and reassuring.

'Are you sure? He just seems to be avoiding me lately, and I …' Sara swallowed hard and went quiet.

'Promise, he's fine—just last night he took me out to dinner, and he was saying how much he's gonna miss you when you're away. So trust me, he's still into you.' OK, things just crossed over into the weird zone. Talk about gag reflex. Brother/girlfriend feelings, not something a sister needs to think about.

'OK then, when you see him tell him I love him and to call me.' Sara sounded as though she was about to cry.

Chicks, Starlah thought, shaking her head as though she wasn't one herself. 'Sure, I'll kick him in the butt and tell him to call you. Have a safe trip. I hope you enjoy your time with your mum.' She hung up.

Still clutching her phone she decided to try and get Daniel. She dialled his number, half expecting it to go to message bank, but he answered it.

'Hey, what's up?' Daniel's voice sounded out of breath.

'Oh hi, I didn't expect you to answer—sorry.' She didn't know what to say now that she had him on the phone.

'OK, so I answered. What do you want?' He sounded annoyed.

'Um yeah, was wondering where you were.' She rubbed her throat, trying to get the lying high pitch out of it.

'Told you I was meeting up with Sara for lunch.' He sounded as though he was walking fast.

Starlah's heart raced; she'd had enough of his lies. 'Really, well that's kinda weird now, coz Sara's been trying to ring you and she just called me to see if I knew where you were. So not cool.' She hung up without saying goodbye, the first time she had done that to anyone. She didn't even feel guilty about it. Not yet anyway.

She threw her phone for the second time in less than ten minutes and argued with herself about the merits of getting rid of it permanently. It only seemed to bring her lies and annoyance anyway. When it rang the third time she walked away from it and locked herself in her room.

Not interested, she slammed the door and fell onto her bed face first, yelling into the pillow. When she released all her frustration she rolled over and closed her eyes. Having only slept briefly last night she allowed the heaviness of her lids to take her back into Slumber Land, too exhausted to resist.

SAIMIRA, WAKE up, the chores hath not the ability to perform their selves,' Jacob's grating voice punctured her slumber. 'Arg Jacob, be gone with you. I hath nay need for a rooster call. Moder assented to my leisure day.' Saimira rolled over and tried to ignore her brother. Sundays were her only day to sleep in past the sunrise. But Jacob thrived on messing with her leisure day. It was like his blood would boil if she were to be given the freedom to enjoy but one day of her week's routine.

'Yea, but I hath need of your early rise. My garments will not mend their selves. Rise and attend to them.' He kicked her foot and smirked at her.

She spun her head around and glared at him. 'Nay, I will not. A maidservant I am not, and I hath nay need to be at your beck and call.' She turned back around and hugged the blanket close to her chin.

'Jacob, leave Saimira be. I will attend to your garments after breakfast,' their mother whispered so as not to wake their father, who rested soundly, snoring in the corner of the room on a straw mat.

'Aye Moder. Sorry I have wakened you.' Jacob lowered his head and quietly walked out of their cottage to attend to the livestock.

Saimira closed her eyes, took a few deep breaths and willed herself to fall back to sleep. She had another hour before she had to help her mother prepare breakfast, but her blood boiled with fury. She didn't know how much longer she could endure Jacob's bothersome manners. She wished that he would find himself a wife and be gone from their family home. But she doubted any such woman existed who would put up with his ugly head.

She sung a lullaby in her mind to try and calm herself down. After a few minutes her body relaxed, and she drifted off back to sleep. She reopened her eyes after what felt like a few minutes and heard her mother fixing breakfast in the small kitchen. She rose and put away the mattress and bedding, and washed her hands and face in a small ceramic bowl before joining her mother in the kitchen.

Her mother was stirring a large pot over a wood stove. She inhaled deeply and savoured the smell of the cooking porridge. She loved the way her mother flavoured the porridge with cinnamon sticks, a Sunday luxury; other days they were allowed but a drizzle of honey.

'Good morn, Moder. Sorry I hath risen late.'

'Hush child, I mind not. I take comfort in watching your

face rest so peacefully.' She walked over to her daughter and embraced her softly against her ample bosom.

Saimira closed her eyes and enjoyed her mother's affection. 'Thanks Moder, I am most grateful.' She smiled and pulled away. 'These smells make my mouth water with envious yearning.'

Her mother smiled. 'Wake your fader and fetch you broder, and we can partake of breakfast.' Her mother finished stirring the porridge and grabbed the bowls, getting ready to pour out four servings.

Saimira went to the corner of the small room and gently shook her father's shoulder. 'Fader, time hath come for breakfast.' She waited as he stirred and then rolled over.

'Good morn, thanks.' He sat up, stretched his arms above his head and jumped up onto his feet.

Saimira attended to packing up the mattress and putting away the bedding before pouring some more hot water into the bowl so her father could wash his hands and face. Then she went to retrieve Jacob, who was out in the fields attending to the livestock. She wrapped a woollen shawl around her shoulders and donned her boots before racing out of the cottage to track down Jacob. She knew that she would find him with his 'kin', she giggled. He would give her a serious hiding if he heard her make such remarks about him, but she cared not.

Sometimes she had to admit she baited him simply because he thought himself so above her and others. She felt the need to keep him levelled for his and her own sake.

She spotted Jacob walking towards her carrying a bucket in each hand. 'Breakfast, Jacob,' she called out to him.

He simply nodded and proceeded to the barn out to the side of their cottage to drop off the supplies.

She took that as cue to race back to the cottage. She hoped that her bowl would still be nice and warm by the time she got to eat it. Maybe this morning her parents would let her eat before she had to wait for Jacob to finish, and if that meant she had to sit on the floor she cared not.

She eagerly burst through the door, hurriedly took off her boots and rewashed her hands. She stood by their humble table and looked down at her father, who was about to eat his first bite.

He looked at her and stopped, then laughed. 'Saimira, your spirit is most lively. I cannot bear to say nay to you. Eat, child, I am sure Jacob will be able to overcome this lapse of routine.'

She grabbed her bowl and felt the warmth seep into her hands. She closed her eyes and sucked in the deepest breath, savouring the cinnamon tickles up her nose. 'Thanks, Fader.' She didn't wait too long before scooping the porridge into her watering mouth, in case Jacob would dare to interrupt her joy. As she scrapped the remaining dregs from the bowl Jacob opened the door. She jumped up and walked into the kitchen to wash her bowl.

He stood at the door and glared at the scene in front of him. 'I see you hath forgotten my existence and proceeded. Nice to see Saimira enjoying breakfast after her heavy duties in the field.' His face burned.

'Come now, Jacob, mind not your sister. I hath given her permission this morn.' Their father smiled.

He hesitated at the door for a few moments, staring at Saimira, and then cast his eyes down, 'Aye, Fader.' He proceeded to wash up and then sat at the table while their mother placed his bowl in front of him. She ran her hand affectionately through his thick, dark wavy hair.

'Ah, my son hath grown so handsome and stout. I imagine a young lady hath caught your eye by now and making your own home is foremost in your mind.' She smiled at him.

His face reddened as he cast his eyes down. 'Nay Moder, nay such lady hath come forth.' He spooned porridge into his mouth and kept his eyes down.

'What hath you to say about Madeline? She is a handsome woman with good familial line.' Their mother persisted.

Saimira's heart quickened. *Nay!* she screamed in her head. Her affection for Madeline's younger brother Simon played through her heart. If Jacob married Madeline he would forever be in her life. That she could not endure.

'I think not, Madeline is not for courting. I believe she hath fixed her eyes on Michel, from Second Village North.' Saimira tried to disguise her heart's lie. Simon's face warmed her. His blue eyes stirred her young heart with electric flutters of pure, innocent delight. His friendship and silliness alleviated her discord with her mundane routine at home and her constant annoyance with Jacob.

'And how hath you such privilege? I daresay your affectionate friendship with Simon hath something do with it.' Jacob glared at her once again. It seemed lately that was all his face was able to do when looking at her.

Saimira's face blazed volcano red. 'Hush, Jacob, you know not my friendships.' She turned her face so her parents couldn't see her. She felt her hands tremble. She was so sick of Jacob spying on her and interfering with her life.

Her mother studied her a moment and turned her attention back to Jacob. 'Jacob, the quest was yours.' When he didn't answer she continued, 'Nay bother. One day soon I shall be singing at your marital union. This I am sure of.' She kissed him on the side of his head and ruffled his hair.

He pulled his head away, but smiled back at his mother with warmth. 'Yea, one day, Moder … one day.'

TWENTY

'STARLAH, WAKE up.'

She felt her shoulder being rocked. 'Go away, Jacob.'

'Jacob? Who's Jacob? Ooh, Starlah's got a boyfriend.'

Starlah sat up, darting her eyes around the room, trying to shake out the brain fog. 'What—what's going on? Oh Daniel, it's you. What are you doing here?' She tried to clear the confusion from her head.

'Of course it's me, who were you expecting? Jacob?' he teased.

She swung her legs over the edge of the bed and sat there, rubbing her eyes. 'No one, just having a weird dream.' She ran her hand through her hair. It was even more matted than before.

'So who's Jacob? Or is that not a question I should ask?' He grinned at her.

'Nay—I mean no—whatever. Leave me alone.' She jumped

up off the bed, remembering that she was still angry with him.

'Nay? Seriously, Starlah, sometimes I think you're from a different century.' He frowned at her. 'Should I be worried about you?' He continued to stare at her.

'N-O, as in "no". I'm fine. You just woke me from a weird dream. Stop the interrogation, will ya?' She caught a glimpse of herself and jumped. No wonder he was worried about her. She ran both hands down her hair and smoothed the sides behind her ears.

He continued to study her and then shook his head. 'What's up with you going all banshee on me?' He stood facing her. 'So I hadn't gotten around to answering a few phone calls from my girlfriend. Don't see how that should be a big deal for you.'

She took a deep breath and then sighed. 'Daniel, enough of this bullshit. Seriously, man up and tell the truth.' She stared into his eyes for a few intense seconds before he looked away. 'You can't expect people to know you're lying and to go along with it. It's doing my head in.' Tears burned her eyes.

He sighed and dropped onto her bed, casting his eyes down. 'I hate the fact I've dragged you into this. But if I tell you what's going down, then your life is in danger. The people I have to do this thing for aren't playing games. Seriously, they'd take us out without even blinking the blood from their eyes.' He rubbed his head and kept his eyes down. 'You just gotta trust me, that I'm gonna take care of things and that I'll be OK. Davo's got my back. OK?' He finally looked up into her eyes.

She studied him a moment and then sat down next to him. 'Fine, you want me to trust you, well then you have to give me something. I don't care if that puts me in danger. I probably already am anyway.' She grabbed his hand and squeezed hard. 'What does "Red Diamond" mean?' She swallowed hard, waiting for him to erupt. She felt his body stiffen.

'How—what the hell, Starlah?' His eyes looked frightened. He let go of her hand, stood up and paced around the room. 'Man, if anyone knows that you even know that—fuck, we're done.' He moved around the room erratically. 'Shit, I gotta let Davo know—I should get you out of here. Where can you stay?' He rambled.

'Whoa, calm down, Danny. No one's going to know anything. I won't mention that word again, promise. And I'm not going anywhere.' Her mouth dried up instantly. OK, maybe she should have kept her nose and the rest of her face out of it. But …

'Starlah, this shit ain't nothing to be joking about. "Red Diamond" it's serious, OK?' He wiped the sweat from his forehead.

She shook off the internal chill squirming through her belly and nodded. 'OK, I'll keep out of it. But I won't stop worrying— sister's duty.' She shrugged then threw her arms around him and forced a hug onto him.

He finally allowed her hug to defrost him and put his arms around her and squeezed tight. 'I just don't know what the hell I'd do if anything happened to you.' She felt a quiver rock his body.

She let a single, pent-up tear escape. 'Likewise.' She managed to stop the rest that threatened to follow suit. She had a flashback to Brad's tormenting phone call and shivered. She hoped that

Brad was running on empty threats, but what if he wasn't? If anything happened to her Daniel would go nuts.

But what was she going to do about Brad? Should she call the cops or just ignore him? Maybe she should call Bella and get her to talk to him. Nah, that wasn't gonna happen.

She felt crestfallen. She missed Bella's wild personality. The ouch factor at the loss of her was way bordering trillions-plus. By now her heart should be immune to such letdowns but it wasn't. Each time someone rejected her, each time someone abandoned her, it hurt like being stabbed with a rod immersed in acid. Yeah, ouch indeed.

Lately she found herself reflecting on her life. How was it that she managed to score such crappy parents, and how come she always found herself in the deep end of the cesspit? Was life really based on a punishment/reward system? Did the wheel of karma really exist?

If it did then she must have done something incredibly horrid to be rewarded with this life. She sighed. She had a weird feeling that Saimira chick had somehow played a part in this. *Yeah thanks, medieval skank, thanks for the nightmare life.*

She saw Saimira's young eyes staring at her from the past— her frightened, haunted eyes and felt a deep sadness wash over her. OK, maybe she shouldn't be so hard on the poor girl. Maybe she should give her the benefit of the doubt. She had a flash of the bloodied rock. Or maybe she shouldn't. She shook.

'You OK?' Daniel pushed her out and studied her.

She inhaled until her shoulders touched her ears and then blew out hard. 'Sure, I'm good.' Nothing to be freaking out over: her brother was up to his neck in murky crap. Her ex-best friend's brother wanted to drive her crazy and maybe dismember her, not to mention her ghostly friend from the past. So yeah, she was all good.

'Sweet, so we'll forget you sticking your cute little nose where it don't belong and move on, hey.' He smiled at her.

She swallowed the protest and smiled back. 'Sure, but you better ring Sara back and tell her all's good with the two of you. I don't want to be the go-between for the two of you. On the gag-o-meter, that's way up there.' She mockingly stuck her finger in her mouth and pretended to gag.

'Will do …' he laughed and shook his head. 'You always make me laugh. Don't ever change.' He ruffled her hair, got tangled in there and fought to free his hand. 'Man, that's some mean dreadlocks you're working on there.' He walked out of her room, laughing.

Starlah initially laughed with him but then frowned. *Hey!*

STARLAH RESTED her head against the wall and let the pounding water from the turbocharged showerhead ease the stress from her tight muscles. She allowed herself these few moments of peace to rejuvenate her body and mind. Tilting her head back she held her breath as the water struck her face, massaging her facial muscles.

She let out a loud 'Ahhh' before it was drowned out by the water filling her mouth. She spat out the water as she ran her hands down her smooth, silky hair. For a change it wasn't a matted mess.

She reluctantly turned the water off and stood there, allowing the water to drip off, before grabbing the towel and vigorously rubbing it over her body. She felt relaxed and revitalised, ready to face her life again.

She heard her phone beeping in the lounge room as she dried

her hair. She ignored it. She didn't want to re-join her life just yet.

'Hey Starlah, phone.'

'Yeah, don't worry about it. I'll check it in a minute,' she yelled from behind the closed door. She swallowed hard, hoping it wasn't 'him' again.

She finished up beautifying herself and went to retrieve her phone. She picked it up and just held it for a few seconds, seeing if she could sense whether it was him or not. She turned it on and was surprised to find a text from Bella.

Hey Starlah, need to talk to you. Can we meet tomorrow at 4 pm at my parent's beach house? Do you remember the one we went to last year for the week?

She reread the message a few times. There was something about it that just didn't seem right, but she was so relieved that Bella wanted to talk to her that she was prepared to ignore that annoying feeling.

Hi Bella, would love to catch up. I've missed you. Sure, I remember where your parents' beach house is. See you there at 4 pm, looking forward to it.

Maybe Bella had time to think things through and was ready to hear her out. Maybe, or maybe she wanted to beat her up. Whatever she wanted Starlah was prepared to risk it, so she had an opportunity to see her again and try to explain things. It had been driving her nuts not being able to talk to Bella.

She went back to her room to finish up before going back out to the lounge room, expecting Daniel to be there, but he wasn't. She heard him rummaging in his room. She noticed that he left his phone on the coffee table. A thought hit her: she should switch on his GPS tracker so the next time he went out to do Davo's errands she would be able to track him down. *Brilliant idea.*

Yeah OK, so she told him she would keep out of it, but sometimes you have to do what you think is right and hope for the best, right? She fumbled with his phone, switched on the tracker and then nearly dropped it as she hurriedly put it back, hopefully exactly where she had found it. She was becoming a pro in sneaking around, just like her big bro. *Not something to be proud of,* whispered her conscience. *Shut up, Jiminy,* she ordered, expecting to see a dancing cricket on her right shoulder. She shook her head—*Losing it.*

Daniel's phone chirped, indicating a message. Starlah wanted to read it, but then he'd know for sure what she had been up to. Instead she yelled out, 'Hey, that's your phone.'

Daniel came out of his room flustered and red-faced. He stormed up to his phone and read the message. 'Freaking great.' He shoved his phone into his pocket and grabbed his keys. 'Gotta split. I'm gonna be back late. Don't go snooping around in my room.' He pointed at her.

'Like I would anyway.' She darted her eyes around the room as guilt tickled the back of her throat.

'Yeah, like you just magically came up with Red Diamond on your own.' He tried to look serious.

'Yeah, yeah, I know, sorry about that. The card fell out of your pocket when I knocked your jacket onto the floor.' She rubbed her throat.

'Sure it did. Whatever, just stay out of my room. I mean it. OK?' This time he did look serious.

'Yeah, I promise. Just relax.' She smiled, hoping he believed her. Why did he so desperately want her to stay out of his room? He'd never said that to her before.

He must be hiding something in there for sure, she concluded. But, she did just promise she would stay out of his room, so she would. He never said anything about not following him though.

She waited five minutes before switching on the GPS tracker and ran out to her yellow JAZZ mobile. She slipped on the gravel in the driveway, dropped her phone and cracked the screen. 'Bloody hell,' she yelled, traumatising the five-year-old neighbour who played in her front yard.

Starlah picked herself and her phone up off the ground and grimaced to the shaking little girl. 'I'm sorry, little girl. It's OK. Keep playing.'

The red-faced girl burst into tears and ran crying into her home.

Starlah took that as a cue and jumped into her car, switching on the ignition and taking off as quick as legally possible.

When she was far enough away from the scene of the crime, she pulled over and studied the phone. She could still distinguish the red GPS line from the cracks in the screen and discovered that Daniel had made his way out to the local pub out the back of Whistle Head. Not too far from where she used to live in the Hinterland.

The pub there had a reputation as being the local hangout for the Zarbura MC. They weren't exactly known as law-abiding citizens. The nightly news often had some snippet about their wrongdoings. She wondered what the hell Daniel was doing there.

She drove past slowly, darting her eyes around the front of the place. It was a small nondescript pub, tucked off the main road and bordering bushland. She couldn't see Daniel, but she eyed off the Harley Davidson conga line and shivered.

She pulled up to the side parking lot and killed the engine. She sat in the car for a while and debated with herself about her right to be there. From where she sat she could see the front entrance.

She held her breath every time the front door swung open, as though she was expecting some monstrous beast to come torpedoing towards her. She let off out nervous giggle. It echoed and sounded out of place in the small car interior.

She sucked in a stale breath and then blew on her numb fingers. She had been gripping the steering wheel so tightly her fingers stopped receiving blood supply. She pumped life back into them, took a deep breath and swung the car door open.

As she put one foot out of the car door the front door to the pub slammed open, and Daniel stormed out. He was followed by two burly guys wearing leather vests with the Zarbura logo on it, the three of them exuding power and aggression. Starlah cringed.

'Oh shit,' she whispered, tucking her foot back into the car. She sat there frozen, staring at Daniel, who was also wearing a Zarbura leather vest. 'What the hell?' She went back to gripping the steering wheel, her fingers resuming their vigilant pose. Her blood pulled away from her fingers again and rushed to her heart. It swelled and protested by bouncing around her ribcage.

She wondered if this was the deep dark secret Daniel was keeping. OK sure, she never expected him to be involved in a motorbike club, but it wasn't really a life-and-death situation for her, surely. There had to be more to it.

She sat there, studying the scene playing out in front of her. Daniel looked right at home amongst the other two members. His body posture had changed. He stood with his legs wide apart, chest puffed out and hands in his jeans pocket. He even held his face more severely. *Which Daniel was the real one?*

Her fingers trembled, pulsing against the steering wheel, as she watched him grab one of the other guy's shirts and shove him up against the wall. She couldn't hear what he was saying, but he had metamorphosed into Mr Agro.

Maybe Danny wasn't who she thought he was. Her eyes watered. 'What the hell are you doing?' She peeled her hands off the steering wheel and wiped at the tears.

She rested her head against the steering wheel and closed her eyes. The one person in her life that she wanted to trust with all her heart appeared to be living a double life. Her stomach sank to the floor of the car and pooled out into a bloodied, seeping mess. Along with her soul. Why not? It might as well.

She felt a heaviness pressing down on her. Was there no one in this world that she could truly trust and rely on? A deep chasm opened up in her heart, and the all-pervasive sinking feeling she felt on the day she tried to end it all seeped back into her heart and mind. She was totally alone in this world.

Sure, she had Jasmine and a version of Daniel. Whether that was the true version or not, she didn't know. What she did know was that there wasn't anyone she could look in the eye and know without a doubt that they were who they said they were.

Her pendant heated up. She didn't even have it in her to clutch it. Even her love for Ardaleigh couldn't take away the sinking feeling swirling through her. What was the point anyway? He was in some other dimension, probably about to be sent to live a life somewhere in this world, and then he would be lost to her, too.

The top of her head tingled. She gritted her teeth and swallowed the pain wanting to burst out of her. 'Go away, leave me alone,' she ordered the empty car. 'You can't help me. You can't even show yourself to me. What good is having a guardian that can't even communicate with me?' She exhaled the sob building in her chest and allowed herself to cry. 'Just go.'

The pendant cooled, and she felt him withdrawing. Now she was truly alone. She was about to allow herself to fall deeper into the pit, but a tap on the window jolted her back. She sprung her head up and just about peed herself—literally—there may have been a tiny leakage.

She locked the door and cracked open the window a fraction. 'What?' she asked the looming male figure.

He leaned into the car and whispered, 'Starlah, what the hell are you doing here? You need to leave now.'

She squinted, trying to make out whose face was peering down at her. Then it finally registered. 'Dave? What the hell?'

'Listen kiddo, it's not safe for you to be here. Seriously, you need to go. Now.' He darted his eyes around the place while trying to conceal his body behind her diminutive car. He would've looked rather comical if it wasn't for the seriousness in his voice.

'But what about Danny? What's happening?' She spun her head around to look at the front door, where Danny had been standing a few moments ago. He was no longer there. 'Where did he go?' Fear rose up her throat and gripped it tight, making her voice sound whiny.

Dave squatted down and indicated for her to drop the window. She did as she was ordered. 'Listen carefully, Danny's doing something really important right now. There's no room for any fuckups, which include his kid sister busting in on him, right? So you need to back up your little car and go home. I promise I'll keep an eye on him and get him home to you, but right now he's doing this thing for me.' He stared into her eyes with such seriousness it made the back of her neck bristle.

She turned the ignition on and for a few moments stared at him. When her eyes could no longer engage in the stare-down, she let her mouth flap. 'You'd better or I'll make sure the cops know you had something to do with whatever's going down here.' She wanted to growl at him but decided against it.

He laughed. 'Righto, feel free to do so. Now go.' He stood up and jogged back to his charcoal grey Jeep with heavily tinted windows, which was parked in the back of the semi-deserted parking lot.

She put her car into gear and reluctantly drove off. As she passed the front of the pub she darted her eyes around, desperately trying to find Daniel. He was nowhere to be seen. Her hands continued to tremble as she pulled away and drove back home. She would have to believe he was coming home soon and would wait patiently for him to return to her, hopefully in one piece.

She parked in the driveway and dragged herself out of the car and up to the front door. She looked over at the neighbour's window and noticed the mum of the little girl pulling back the blinds. She simply waved, mouthed, 'sorry' and let herself in.

Everything felt difficult to do: the key had trouble turning in the lock. The door weighed more. Her feet felt as though they had Velcro on the bottom of her shoes. Even breathing required her to remember how to do it.

She dropped the keys to the floor and shuffled forward. She stood, shoulders drooping, and stared at the cabinet where Daniel kept his booze. She wanted to shuffle her feet over to the cabinet, grab the biggest bottle of liquor and pour it down her gullet like a baby pigeon guzzling down its regurgitated meal.

But she didn't have it in her. She fell onto the sofa, curled up into a ball and hugged the cushion tight to her chest. She buried her face into the soft fabric and let loose silent tears, praying Daniel would burst through the door any minute.

TWENTY-TWO

ARDALEIGH STOOD back and watched Starlah crumble to the sofa. His heart ached that he couldn't do anything to console her. She had made it clear, she didn't want him around. He watched her body emanate colours of deep pain and permeate his own body with its sorrow. He twirled his pendant and breathed through the pain. He held back his energy so she wouldn't feel his presence.

She lifted her head off the pillow and wiped her eyes. He held his breath as she darted her eyes around the room, momentarily forgetting that she couldn't see him. She sat up and smoothed down her golden hair. He loved how self-conscious she was about her sometimes unruly hair.

He resisted the desire to run his fingers through it. The memories of him burying his fingers in her hair, pulling back her head and kissing her taunted him. His lips tingled.

She stood up and paced around the room. She walked up to the front door, opened it and stared out into the darkness. After a few minutes, she slammed the door shut and resumed pacing. She walked past Ardaleigh and stopped.

Could she sense him? He withdrew his energy, almost to the point of returning to the Fourth Realm. He shimmered on the threshold. Her fused brow and distressed aura held him there.

He debated with himself; maybe he should just return to the Fourth Realm and give her the space she demanded. The irresistible pull she had on him kept him grounded in her realm; his whole being pulsated with pain and indecision.

The front door burst open, and Daniel stormed in. His body emanated red and varying degrees of yellow and grey. The combination of anger and fear oozed off him in palpable waves.

Starlah jumped and clutched her throat. 'Oh Danny, thank God you're OK.' She raced towards him, oblivious to the energy emanating from him. She threw her arms around him and burst into tears.

His body's energy gleamed with orange and green, dispersing the remaining red and grey tones. He threw his arms around her. 'Fuckin' hell, Starlah, seriously, you followed me. What the hell's up with that? You could have gotten both of us fucked up.' He hugged her tight.

'I'm so sorry, Danny, please don't be angry with me.' She didn't let him go. 'I didn't know what else to do. You keep things from me that are obviously dangerous and expect me to not give a shit.' She finally let him go, and wiped at her tears. 'I don't want to lose you—I've just got you back.' Her bottom lip trembled.

He studied her a moment and then sighed. 'Oh, come on. Don't cry. Shit, I hate it when I make you cry.' He stuck out his arm. 'Always did. Remember that time when you were like nine years old and you were snooping around in my room and I totally raged on you? You pulled that pouty trembling lip on me and burst into tears. Man, I felt like a complete arsehole.'

She fell back into Danny's arms. 'Just like now. Sorry, Starbright.' He hugged her.

Ardaleigh watched them exchanging loving energy and knew she was safe. He raised his vibration and left them to talk things over. The Fourth Realm was but a thought away. All he had to do to return home was increase his vibration and use his mind.

He now found himself standing in his white, dome-shaped house and felt momentarily disorientated, as he tried to shake off the tingling sensation through his body. Sometimes, flipping from one realm to another had some unsettling effects as the body readjusted to the higher frequency. When he had to lower his vibration to adjust to the Third Realm, he also suffered the same readjusting sensation as the density of his light body increased. But that was worth it, if it meant that he could be in Starlah's presence.

There was a tap at the door. He walked up to the door and swung it open. 'Sister Katalin, so nice to see you. Please, come in.' He stepped back so she could walk in.

'Thank you, Ardaleigh,' she spoke informally as she stepped into his domain. 'How is Younger Sister Starlah?' she surmised, as the afterglow of his return still lingered on the outskirts of his aura.

'She appears to get herself into one troubling event after another. Sometimes, I wonder if my words penetrate her mind at all. She is the most stubborn and difficult subject I've ever watched over.' He smiled.

'Ah yes, good to see nothing has changed,' she laughed. 'She always was a strong-willed one.' She walked through the small open-plan living area and turned to face him. Her strawberry-blonde hair hung in beautiful waves down her back. Her iridescent blue eyes sparkled with concern and apprehension.

Ardaleigh eyed her with trepidation. 'Please, have a seat,' he said.

She took a seat in one of the hand-carved, solid-wood armchairs, decorated down the arms and legs with stunning patterns of swirls and flowers. She lifted the hem of her pale pink, silk gown, crossed her legs and placed her hands on her knee.

He braced himself. 'Just say it, Sister Katalin; I cannot bear the hesitation any longer.' He swallowed hard, waiting for her to speak. He sat in the chair opposite her and crossed his legs, mirroring her.

'Very well, Tomace has submitted his petition for your rebirthing, with additional evidence to support his notions. He seems to have convinced at least two other members of the elders.' She looked directly into his eyes. Her eyes held compassion. 'I am afraid that I am not hopeful for the rejection of the petition this time, Ardaleigh. I want you to be prepared.' She raised her hand and fiddled with her pendant.

His stomach dropped. Flashes of Starlah raced through his

mind. He crushed his pendant in his hand. His impulse was to run away, but where could he run to that the Guild could not follow? Hiding was futile. All members of the Harper Guild were connected through their Bludlin bond.

'Are you all right?' Katalin asked, as though not knowing the answer. 'This may be a painful notion for you, but once you are rebirthed, you will not remember this pain and your life will be one of joy. I believe a nice family may have already been set aside if the vote is passed.' She reached over and placed her delicate hand on his knee.

He emulated a statue. The idea of not remembering his love, the notion of being away from his twin flame for another cycle, was too much to bear. His heart squeezed with pain; breathing was a second thought.

'Not remember. You say it as though it is a good thing. How can it be a good thing, Katalin?' He dropped formality and stared into her eyes with intensity. 'How can a life in the Third Realm without Starlah ever be a good thing?' He jumped up.

'I know, Brother Ardaleigh, it is not something that you desire or are willing to accept; however, I'm afraid the decision is up to the Elders. Come the next sun ascension, the Guild are meeting in the Temple. The votes will be cast and you will be summoned for the deliberation. I strongly propose you spend the next few hours making peace with that.'

Katalin stood up and walked over towards him, then stopped. 'I truly am sorry that you are in such pain.' She reached out and her hand hesitated over his shoulder. She pulled back her hand and turned to leave. She paused at the door and sighed.

'Ardaleigh, Tomace is doing this for your own betterment, but I am sorry for the heartache it is causing.' She stepped out, quietly closed the door and left him to his pain.

He trembled as he rested his head against the wall. Was his fate sealed? Was there any point in hoping the other remaining Elders would reject the petition? *Please, let it be.*

Tomace's face taunted him. What was this additional evidence that he had? There wasn't anything concrete that Ardaleigh could think of that would make a rebirth definite but in Tomace's mind it must be conclusive. He hoped the others wouldn't think it so.

He peeled his head off the wall and paced around his home. Most Harper Guild homes were of the same structure and layout. Other Guilds had their unique designs to designate their domains.

The bricks were white limestone. Inside, areas were sectioned off by one metre high walls of the same limestone, so his bedroom was partitioned off slightly from the kitchen area. The only room completely closed off from the other areas was the grooming chamber.

He walked around the wall, stared at his bed and wondered if he would be able to force sleep upon himself. He eyed off his comfortable large bed, but doubted the softness and relaxation his mattress normally provided would relieve the pain swirling through his heart and mind.

He sat on the bed anyway and hoped that the special design of the mattress would comfort him. The materials used to create the mattress were unique to this realm. The soft, conforming mattress, created from the leaves of a samkubular tree, reacted to the warmth of the body. Its particles continue to oscillate even when redesigned into a mattress and allowed for a fluid motion under the body, almost like a waterbed from the Third Realm, only more interactive and comforting for the body.

He turned to look at the hematite orb sitting on the bedside table. He grabbed it and held it close to his chest. It hummed warmly against his hands. The orb pulsed, reacting to his touch, and after a few moments burst into a hologram projection, casting lifelike images of Starlah and himself. The image captured with Ardaleigh behind Starlah, wrapping his strong arms around her. Both of them were smiling deeply, completely content and in love.

He reached his hand out to trace his fingers across her cheek, but it went straight through, the distorted image a reminder of the truth. He dropped the orb back onto the table, and as it cooled, the image withdrew back into its centre, keeping their image safe until the next time he could hold and unlock it.

He didn't know what to do. He wanted this day to be done with, but he knew he should spend the next few hours preparing his defence. However, if Tomace had his way, then nothing he said would make any difference.

Starlah's beautiful smile echoed through his mind, convincing him to at least try. He grabbed the crystal slate, resembling a tablet device, and dictated his rationale for not being rebirthed. The device responded to the vibration of his voice, transcribing as he spoke.

He looked over what he had prepared and his heart sank. He

had nothing convincing beyond his love for Starlah, and loving someone was never acceptable justification.

He threw the crystal slate onto the bed. It bounced off and landed onto the hard wooden floor, cracking the screen. He watched the liquid crystal ooze out onto the floor, taking with it his flimsy petition. He closed his eyes and took a deep breath. He realised he had no choice but to surrender to his fate. He focused on his breath and on lowering his vibration. *Not without seeing Starlah first.* He concentrated on returning to the Third Realm.

TWENTY-THREE

STARLAH STARED into Danny's eyes as he relayed the night's events to her. At least what he could tell her without jeopardising her life. She kept blinking her eyes as though what he was saying could be blinked away.

'Red Diamond is kinda code for the new synthetic drugs hitting the streets. They're like what they call "bath salts", if you've heard of that, only tainted red with "red diamond snake venom". But I doubt it's real venom, hey,' he said as though that made it better. 'Davo's got me hooking back up with the Zarburas so I can get in on the next run.' He looked pale and tired.

She continued to stare at him between blinking spasms. Her mouth fell open, like a stupefied zombie trying to catch flies. She couldn't believe he was actually involved with criminals dealing this crazy new drug. *Why Daniel?*

He stopped talking and looked at her with concern. 'Are you

OK? Told ya you didn't want to know.' He jumped up onto his feet and paced around. 'But it ain't what you think. I'm not really … I want you know that I'm only doing this coz I owe Davo. When this run is done, I'm out for real.' He stopped and glanced at her; he seemed to cringe with guilt.

Not only was Daniel a bikie, but he was also involved with drugs. *Great,* she thought. *His life story just keeps on getting better.*

She shook her head and put her face into the palm of her hand. 'I seriously don't know how to react.' She lifted her face and stared at him. 'You better get your freaking shit together and grow up, unless you want to end up back in jail.'

He remained quiet with his head down. A cloak of defeat appeared to envelop him. Why he didn't just get out now she couldn't understand. Why did he let Davo dictate to him, and why did he look so sad?

'Yeah you're right, if I had a choice I'd put this crap behind me but …' He turned and walked towards his room. 'I'm tired. I'm gonna hit the sack. Love ya, Starbright, hope you can forgive me.'

He closed the door to his room, leaving Starlah standing there confused and overwhelmed. None of what he was doing made any sense. This Daniel didn't resemble the bikie Daniel she had seen earlier. His distraught body language didn't match his actions.

She rubbed her temples hard. She didn't know how much more turbulence she could endure. Surely there was a saturation point? The silence in the lounge room was becoming eerily painful. She gazed at her watch. It was past midnight.

She walked up to Daniel's room and put her ear against the door. He was snoring. How the hell could he fall asleep so easily? Surely, he should be tossing and turning as much as she knew she would be. Oh well, she shrugged, no point in loitering around his door. It's not like anything was going to change by her being a door stalker.

She retired to her room. Maybe the morning would be better. Hopefully, she pleaded even though she knew it was useless. She had asked the same thing the day before and the day ended up— well, not better.

She remembered Bella's message and shivered. The thought of meeting up with her caused her nerves to fire off in all directions at once. The experience of having to face what Bella's brother had done was not on her list of 'most anticipated events'. God, she hoped Bella wouldn't look at her with accusatory eyes. *Please keep an open mind, Bells.* Her throat tightened.

She stood over the basin and splashed cold water onto her face. The cold greeted her skin like a slap across her face. She welcomed it, offering it up as penance. In some distorted way she felt as though she deserved it. It didn't do much for relieving the tension though, so she laid down on her bed and bartered with the counting sheep for sleep.

Saimira's heart quickened as she made her way through the green fields to meet up with Simon. She pictured his ultramarine blue eyes sparkling in the sunlight, as though they held the mirror lake's essence. She had tried many times to get him out of her mind and failed. She questioned herself; did she really want to extract him from her heart or mind? *Nay, most definitely not!*

Maybe today he would be brave and ask if he could court her. She was old enough now. Most girls were wedded by their fifteenth year. So she figured they could court for a year and wed a year later. She would be almost fifteen by then. Surely her parents would consent. Oh, how blessed she would feel.

Her heart pounded in her ears as she approached the final bend in the pathway before making her way to the lake, where Simon would be there to greet her with his endearing smile.

She hitched up her dress and jogged the last few yards. She stopped when she saw him sitting on a boulder by the lake, throwing pebbles into the water, sending cascading ripples through the mirror reflection on the water. The sky's image glistened across the water as the ripples distorted the image momentarily and then resettled to reveal its crystal clear beauty.

He spun his head around when he heard her puffing as she approached. 'Aye, Saimira hath shown. Greetings.' He jumped to his feet and went over to greet her. He stopped in front of her and hesitated a moment before leaning in and giving her a quick, awkward hug. He pulled away and ran his hands down his burgundy tunic while looking down at the ground. His cheeks heated up.

'And greetings to you Simon—so nice to see you.' She played down her excitement. Her face gave away nothing, but her heart pounded giddily. 'I see the poor lake hath received your pebble wrath.' She smiled cheekily at him.

'Aye, 'tis what you get if you cross Simon, the Lord of Harring Borough.' He dipped down, scooped up a handful of tiny pebbles and raised them in mock assault. 'You get the pebble wrath.' He carefully threw a few pebbles Saimira's way.

She feigned insult. 'Arh, you wretched beast.' Giggling, she bent down and picked up her own assault pebbles and threw them his way before running. 'You are most certainly not a lord of any borough or even a hare's warren.'

He gave chase and they both giggled, running around the lake's edge. He was almost upon her.

She turned her head to look over her shoulder and didn't see a bigger rock jutting out from the rest of the rocks. She tripped over it, twisted her ankle and came crashing down, landing on her knees. She cried out, rolled over and sat there holding her knees, biting her bottom lip, not wanting to cry.

Simon ran to her and dropped to his knees to inspect her. 'Do you fare well? 'Tis a spectacular tumble.' His face wavered between concern and humour.

'You truly are a wretched beast.' She frowned at him while rubbing her knees through the material of her peach bliaut dress. She noticed blood seeping through the material. 'Oh, Moder will be most upset. I have ruined my new clothes.' She verged on the threshold of bursting into tears but didn't want to look like a child in front of Simon.

Simon's face took on a more concerned expression when he noticed the blood, and he reached over and grabbed the bottom of her dress, lifting it to expose her knees.

She sucked in a breath, grabbed the front of her bodice and

scrunched it tight. Her heart galloped. She forgot about the pain and blood and the fact her mother would be cross with her, and she focused on his touch.

He tenderly traced his finger around the edges of the bleeding skin and pursed his lips. 'Ooh, looks rather painful—told you to be careful of my pebble wrath—all the pebbles unite, you know.' He looked into her eyes, and she couldn't help but burst out laughing.

'You are most horrid, Simon Tailorson. Some days I have to wonder why I bother with you.' She smiled through her frown.

'Aye, 'tis my handsomeness that keeps you coming back.' He grinned.

'More like your beastly looks make me feel sorry for you.' She picked up some dirt and threw it at his chest.

He laughed heartily. 'Aye, they always did say you love to hang with beasts.' He dusted the dirt off across his chest. 'I didn't think they were talking about me.'

'Yea, 'tis you my friend they refer to.' Her cheeks burned brighter than the sun's aura. He left his finger hovering above her knee, sending electric currents up her thighs, converging in her hidden parts. She gasped and squirmed, feeling betrayed by her body's desires, and had to focus hard on not giving away her feelings.

His face turned serious. He darted his eyes from her exposed legs to her face. His breathing became more hurried and audible. He gazed into her eyes, questioning them with his intensity. He lowered his finger and traced around the sore and then above her knee.

She thought she was going to burst into to flames. His touch felt like kindle, igniting the flame through her body. Unexpectedly he leaned in, planted a wet peck against her stunned lips and then retreated, looking away red-faced, trembling.

'Sorry,' he blurted, 'my body hath taken a mind of its own.' He looked up into her face and then back around the scenery.

She grabbed his hand, squeezing it. 'Nay need for apologies. I enjoy your affection.' This time she looked away. 'I had hoped you shared my affection and would ask me something.' She looked back up to his face and swallowed hard.

His neck turned red as the heat from his face ventured down. He cleared his throat. 'Ah, I was in wonder at the idea of you and I, maybe we could start to …' he didn't get to finish. They both darted their eyes towards the figure hurtling towards them.

Jacob thundered towards Simon, knocked him over and jumped on top of him, pounding his fist into Simon's young flesh.

Simon tried in vain to buck him off and throw his own fists into Jacob's face, but Jacob's rage infused him with otherworldly strength. He kept pounding fiercely into Simon's face, turning it into a purple bloodied mess.

Saimira screamed. 'Nay Jacob, stop, you wretched beast. Please stop.' She grabbed his tunic and tried to pull him off.

He barely noticed her efforts. He growled like an animal and continued on his rampage. 'You dare to violate my kin with your filthy hands. You will pay with your blood.' He grabbed Simon around the throat and squeezed.

Simon's eyes rolled back, and he gurgled and frothed around

the mouth as Jacob squeezed the remaining air from his throat.

Saimira screamed, watching her beloved being taken from her. She felt as though her own life was being drained. A dark cloud descended across her vision. She leaned over and picked up the rock that tripped her and raised it above her head. She looked at Simon's face turning purple, drained of life, and screamed.

The rock smacked into the side of Jacob's skull, sending a loud popping sound throughout the forest; the birds scattered. Jacob fell sideways and slumped onto the ground beside Simon, who lay limp, groaning.

Starlah stood frozen, holding the dripping rock, and stared at the bloody mess in front of her. She trembled all over. Suddenly the rock weighed a tonne and fell from her fingers. She screamed again, ran to Simon and cradled his battered head.

'Oh Simon, please wake up. Please, by the blessed mercy of our Father the Lord, please be with life.' She cradled his head, crying from the depths of her soul. She didn't dare look at her brother, who laid lifeless, blood and brain matter seeping into the water's edge, soiling the beauty of the mirror lake's reflection with its claret hue.

Starlah sat bolt upright in her bed, clutching her throat, screaming. Her whole body trembled violently. She felt her stomach contract and twist. She jumped to her feet and ran to the bathroom, just making it to the sink before projectile-vomiting the nightmare all over the basin and onto the floor.

Her body swayed as the image of the bloodied rock came back to haunt her.

She fell to her knees and sobbed. She was a murderer. She actually killed someone, her brother. Oh my God, it was no wonder she had been punished with this hellish life. She *deserved* it. Her stomach heaved again, but this time she didn't even bother to aim for the sink. She let it flow into the other mess on the floor. She would deal with it later.

She kept her eyes open, but it didn't stop the vivid images of Jacob's brain oozing out or her holding the blood-saturated rock. She knew that Saimira wasn't her as such, but it was her, down at the core of her being. That was even worse, that she was a murderer at the core of her being.

She shook her head forcefully. No, that wasn't true. Saimira did it to save Simon, which made her a hero, not a murderer, right? She wiped the tears and vomit from her face. She couldn't convince herself of that though.

She had been privy to Saimira's fantasies about getting Jacob out of her life, so maybe Saimira had done it deliberately. Maybe a part of her smashed that rock into Jacob's skull with too much force on purpose. Could Saimira have gotten Jacob off Simon without cracking his skull open? She guessed she would never know.

She stood back up and turned on the bathroom light. It momentarily blinded her before her bloodshot eyes adjusted. She looked at her watch; it was 2:30 am. She studied herself in the mirror and cringed at the woeful image.

Her hair flailed around her in that typical fashion she was

becoming accustomed to. Her eyes housed dark pools of despair under them, no longer able to fit all the crap into mere bags. They had been upgraded to crescent-shaped pools. Her once bright mocha brown eyes looked like a swamp had settled in them, murky as all crap.

She turned the water on and washed down the vomit before slapping cold water onto her face. She stuck the plug into the bottom of the sink, filled up the basin with water and then shoved her face into it, the cold biting into her skin. *Bring it,* she mouthed underwater.

Saimira's face greeted her at the bottom of the sink. She looked distraught and haggard. She mouthed 'I am sorry' before disappearing.

Starlah pulled her face up, gasping for air. She stared into the water, expecting to see Saimira's face bobbing up and down in it as water dripped off her own face. But the image had already vanished.

'No, that ain't me,' she told the water sloshing in the sink. 'I'd never do anything to hurt my brother.' She tilted her head back and groaned. 'Seriously, I've had enough of this messed up crap.' She growled through her teeth. 'Why won't everyone leave me the hell alone?'

'Starlah, what the hell's going on?' Daniel stood in the doorway, looking like he was witnessing true madness. He eyed the vomit all over the floor and her wet dripping face and frowned. 'Have you lost the plot or what? What the fuck are you yelling about? And what the hell's this mess? Are you drunk?' He shook his head in disbelief.

She looked at his shocked expression, then at her own image and nodded. 'Yes—exactly, I couldn't sleep, so I downed half a dozen shots, and this is the result.' She waved her hand over the mess on the floor and then her own face.

He looked down at the soiled floor and frowned. 'Suppose you're blaming me for that?' He looked torn.

'Oh no, this one's all me. Don't be guilt tripping Danny. This is all me.' She would've liked to put the blame on his shoulders, but it was her own messed-up self that was responsible. She giggled, adding to the conviction of her losing the plot. 'We truly are one fucked-up family.'

He looked at her and then half-smiled. 'Yeah, you're right. What can we expect, coming from the Rose Clan? Fucked up from birth.' He shook his head and retreated back towards the door. 'Well, I ain't hanging around to help you clean that up.' He pointed to the chunky bits on the floor. 'So I'll leave it to ya— and crazy banshee? Try to get some sleep, will ya?' He walked out of the room, still shaking his head, whispering, 'Fucking Rose genes.'

She watched him leave and nodded, whispering under her breath, 'Yeah, crazy fucked-up Rose genes—no hope there.'

ARDALEIGH STOOD back and watched agony infuse Starlah's body. He hated seeing her so wounded. The Starlah he knew and loved was still hidden in there, under all the mess and vomit.

He observed her scooping up the remnants of her shock, muttering to herself. Even in the pit of despair, she looked beautiful to him. He wanted to help her, but had to settle for standing back and watching her aura change colours with her fleeting emotions.

Wave after wave of different emotions rippled towards him, hitting him in the centre of his being. He welcomed and experienced them with her. He tried sending love and calming energy her way, but she seemed immune to their effects. She had just remembered her past life as Saimira and the heartache from that time.

A cloud of despair and self-hate permeated the air blocking the revelation of the true lesson. If she wallowed in this state for too long, he feared their reunion would be in doubt.

He remembered Tomace and his heart squeezed. That was if he was even there to greet her. He cringed.

She finished cleaning up the mess and herself and went back to bed. She laid her head down tentatively, praying she didn't have to see anymore tonight. He would help her with that. He focused his energy onto the centre of her forehead and bathed her mind with sedating, relaxing waves.

He watched her take a deep breath and visibly relax. She sighed and sunk further into the mattress, hugging her doona. Then she drifted off to sleep. Once the frequencies of her brainwaves were in a relaxed and receptive state, he reached out to her. It was in this state that they could truly connect.

He lay down next to her. She smiled in her sleep. He watched her face change from being clouded with pain to being more relaxed and at peace. His heart brightened. He traced his finger across her cheek. She gasped.

'Starlah, it's me.' He continued to try to coax her. She squirmed and rolled over onto her side, facing him. He leaned in and kissed the middle of her forehead. She reached her arms out and wrapped them around him. His heart responded. He studied her perfect, creamy complexion and rose-tinged cheeks. It upset him how she failed to recognise how beautiful she was.

She resisted accepting his unfaltering love and acceptance of her new form, but the beauty she denied in herself, he embraced with an open heart. Each life journey through the Third Realm brought the soul closer to its true form. With each life, the physical form was brought closer to its true form. The closer to ascension, the closer one united with their perfect, true form. Starlah failed to acknowledge that there was little difference between the two.

Her eyes fluttered opened. 'Mm, that's some way to be greeted. Hello, my love.' She smiled into his eyes. She had made the leap into the astral state, where they could pretend that no other reality existed for a brief moment.

'Hi there, yourself.' He grinned as though he had won the most precious gift. 'That was some performance,' he said.

She cringed. 'Yeah, I know, not my best moment.' She hugged him, resting her face against his chest. 'Truth's revelations hit me pretty hard.' She trembled at the memory.

'Yes, I imagine it would; however, self-hate and self-deprecation aren't why you were sent back, Starlah. Remember that.' He played with her hair.

'Yeah I know. They are the emotions I must learn to transcend.' She looked up into his face. 'It's so hard to break through the fog and understand things. I never remember anything we talk about when we meet here.' She sat up. 'It's so bloody frustrating dealing with the Third Realm buffer.'

He smiled. 'It's equally frustrating for me to try and get through that buffer.'

She leaned in and kissed him. 'Sorry, I know how stubborn I can be, but I don't ignore you deliberately. I just have a hard time connecting or making sense of those annoying stomach butterflies and back tingles. Seriously, how are you supposed to distinguish the difference between … *oh, I'm hungry or get the hell out of here, there's a monster after you?*'

He laughed. 'That's the challenge now, isn't it? We all face that challenge in the Third Realm.' He pulled her in, kissed the top of her head and closed his eyes. Tomace's face taunted him. He knew he would be summoned to the Elders' meeting soon and shivered.

She looked at him and frowned. 'What's the matter?'

He didn't want to worry her and hesitated in telling her the truth. She had enough to deal with, and he was afraid this might push her over the edge. Instead he smiled, rolled her over onto her back and kissed her. 'Not a thing, you're here with me now. That's all that matters.'

'Mm, nice dodge, mister, but I suppose I can go with the flow.' She rolled him back over and kissed him in return.

He wanted to fill his heart with her memory, hoping that he could imprint her all over his DNA, and she would remain with him in his new life. He doubted that would be allowed, but nonetheless he would try.

He buried his face into her hair and inhaled, filling his lungs with the smell of honey and almond. He inhaled until he could no longer fit any air in, directed that memory to a remote part of his brain and seared it into his neurons. When he was satisfied that memory was safe he looked into her eyes, etching their beauty into a different part of his brain.

He rolled her back over onto her back and looked down to her full lips. He closed his eyes and pressed his lips against them, absorbing their essence and storing the memory of their softness and heart-pounding effect in his heart.

He pulled back and scanned his eyes down her neck to the sensual dip at the bottom of her throat, her heartbeat inviting him closer. He traced his burning finger around it, feeling it respond.

He continued to run his finger down the front of her shirt, opening the buttons with one hand. He dipped his hand in and cupped her left breast. The softness and contour ignited his passion. He leaned in and kissed the top curve of her left breast and then did the same with her right one.

She sucked in a breath and arched her back. 'I feel as though you're saying goodbye, but it feels so good. Don't stop.'

He unbuttoned the rest of her shirt, pulled it open and kissed her stomach. Her belly quivered at his touch. He rested his head against her stomach and listened to her heart pounding above. A deep sadness clouded the moment. This would be the last time in a whole lifetime that he would be able to caress her body and fill his heart with her presence.

She ran her fingers through his hair, pulling on it lightly as she lost herself to his touch. 'Oh Ardaleigh, you make it all bearable.' She writhed.

He had to make this memory last. He lay on top of her and kissed her with every essence of his being, allowing his body to speak all the things his mouth couldn't.

TWENTY-FIVE

STARLAH STRETCHED her arms above her head and arched her back. Her eyes fluttered open and greeted the day. *Wow, that was some dream I must have had.* She blinked away sleepy residue. Her body still pulsed with the aftereffects of her night-time interlude.

She ran her finger over her bottom lip, trying to remember why they tingled. Ardaleigh's image was fresh in her mind, and she wondered if he had something to do with it. She smiled; somehow she knew he must have.

She took a deep breath, revelling in the beauty of the day, and a sour stench hit her nose hard—*Eww.* She remembered her 2:30 am performance and cringed. *Aargh, stupid brain, why can't you forget those memories and not the good ones?* She reluctantly swung her legs over the edge of the bed and sat there, rubbing the back of her matted hair. Beautiful as usual, she laughed at herself.

Somehow despite last night's vomit fest she felt peace and a sense of joy. She went into the bathroom, looked down at the floor and frowned. *No, no chunky leftovers are going to disrupt my joy.* She smiled past the mess, washed her face and tried to run a brush through her hair. She gritted her teeth and continued to try to keep the smile on her face as the brush pulled out chunks of her hair.

'What a beautiful day this will be,' she said. 'Right!' She grimaced—well, she was aiming for a smile, but she was sure it looked more like a chimpanzee doing his war expression. She gave up and opened all the windows to her room and bathroom, hoping to air out the remaining odour.

She pulled out the disinfectant and scrubbed the remaining evidence until her bathroom sparkled. It was only then that she felt able to face Daniel. He must think she was a complete nutcase. She went out to the living area to face the inquisition.

He was standing in the kitchen with a cuppa in his hand, facing the window, staring out into the yard. She walked up behind him and took a deep breath. He spun around with wide eyes, probably terrified of what kind of mess he was going to find. He looked relieved when he saw her.

'Morning, how are you feeling? Do you need some painkillers for that hangover?' He had a smirk on his face.

She frowned at first, but then remembered that she had told him she was drunk last night. 'No, I'm good, thanks.' She smiled.

'I dunno. That was some show last night. Sure you don't need nuffin?' He sipped his coffee.

She walked over to the kettle and went about making herself

a strong cup of coffee. 'No, this will hit the spot.' She hoped that he wouldn't ask her many details about last night. There was no way she could share any of it.

He studied her, continuing to sip his coffee, and then asked, 'So do you want to talk about it?'

'Huh, about what?' *Don't ask me … please don't ask me.*

'OK, OK, you don't want to talk about it. That's fine with me.' He looked relieved and didn't push the issue. He had done his brotherly duties and asked, but she could tell that he didn't really want the details.

She smiled, walked up to him and hugged him one-handed, without spilling a drop. 'I love you, Danny. Please be safe, and tell Davo you're done after whatever you owe him is done.'

He put his cup down and hugged her back. 'I will, and then I promise I'll tell you everything. But for now don't worry too much, and please stay out of it. I can't handle dealing with all the Davo crap in addition to worrying about you.' He gave her a big squeeze, and she giggled and spilt half her cup onto the floor.

He let go and looked down to the floor. 'Hm, looks familiar.'

'Shut up, you …' She smiled and flicked a few drops his way.

Laughing he spun around and headed back to his room, and she was left cleaning the mess once again.

TWENTY-SIX

ARDALEIGH, YOU have been summoned by your Bludlin Guild. For what reason do you know?' Katalin looked down at him with pain and sadness.

Ardaleigh swallowed hard and put his head down. 'I do not wish to engage with formality. If a decision has been made then cast it. I cannot bear to play the game.'

He kept his face down and had his hands crossed in front of him. It stopped them from trembling. He heard someone gasp.

'Very well Brother, as you wish.' Tomace looked down at him, getting ready to declare the punishment.

'One moment, Brother. Do not be so quick to cast our Younger Brother here to a rebirth. It is our duty as carers of the Harper Bludlin Guild to measure all and decide on the highest good for all,' the Eldest Brother voiced.

'Yes of course, Eldest Brother. I meant no disrespect.' Tomace looked chastened.

Ardaleigh looked up with hope. Maybe a decision hadn't been decided yet. He darted his eyes around the Elders to see if he could read where they were at. They were indecipherable. His heart pounded.

'Proceed,' the Eldest Brother commanded.

'Yes, very well. Younger Brother, you have been summoned before your Bludlin Guild to examine whether your actions have breached the Fourth Realm's laws and whether you would benefit from another life through the Third Realm,' Tomace said.

Katalin cleared her throat. 'Younger Brother, what do have to say about your actions?' She looked away when she saw his haunted stare.

He reflected for a moment and sighed, 'I have searched my heart and mind trying to come up with some form of defence against being reborn. If loving someone with all of your being is a violation against our laws—then I have no defence.' He looked into each of the Harper Elders' faces and continued.

'Tomace would have me believe that the giving of your heart to another, of doing what you can to protect a member of our Bludlin, even in the Third Realm, is violating some law. I question that, Brothers and Sisters. I question, when is it ever wrong to love unconditionally and fully? When is it against nature's law to protect and guide those we love? When is it unforgivable when you have the power to intercept a violent crime against someone who holds the other half of your soul?'

He looked into the Harper Elder's eyes. 'Eldest Brother, I

know that I have pushed the boundary between our two realms, but why is that wrong? Why can we not be more transparent in our guidance and communication with our loved ones in the Third Realm?' He opened his arms in surrender. 'Why do we hold on to these ancient rules, when we know that many of our soul brothers and sisters are crying out in need?' He dropped his arms at his sides and shrugged. 'If what I say is in direct violation of our nature's law, then I am at your mercy.'

The Eldest Brother leaned forward, almost toppling over the edge of his ascended cathedra, and nodded. 'Thank you, Younger Brother. I thank you for your heart's truth.'

He put his index finger across his lips and thought for a moment. 'Hmm, a difficult one to deliberate. I understand Tomace's petition, and I am receptive to your questions. Our laws are clear; however, you have raised some very important questions about the nature of our laws.'

He frowned and rubbed his forehead. 'But I am not sure this is the correct forum to be deliberating a change in our laws, Young Bludlin.' He looked around at the other ascended Elders and sought their input. 'What do you have to say about these matters, Brothers and Sisters?'

They once again closed themselves off to the gathered assembly below and whispered in their secret language, deciding Ardaleigh's fate. He looked around at the other brothers and sisters of the Harper's Guild and searched their faces for support.

They whispered and murmured among themselves. Some cast frowns, while others nodded in support. He wasn't the only one up for rebirth and he felt his throat tighten. He may have ignited something beyond his simple desire to remain with Starlah.

Many of his brethren had their twin flames reborn, and he knew their hearts beat in unison with his own, while some of the others would be more rigid in their following of the laws.

Amberley, one of his friends in the guild, dared to approach him despite the others oohing and ahhing at her bravery or stupidity, depending on whom they were loyal to. 'Younger Brother, I fear you may have stirred the camp somewhat.' She looked into his eyes and smiled. 'Interesting ideas you propose.' She looked around the assembly and leaned in conspiratorially. 'I think some of the more mature members' hearts are fluttering in shock.' She giggled.

He looked around and nodded, swallowing hard. 'I know, but it was not my intention to "stir the camp", as you say. All I wanted to do was speak my heart's truth.' He looked into her bright blue eyes. 'It seems my heart speaks the truth of more than just my own heartache.'

Amberley nodded. 'Yes, I think so. I have felt the ache and low of being separated from my flame. Ever since Theo was rebirthed I feel as though I live at half pace.' She placed her hand onto his shoulder. 'You have my support.'

He studied her eyes for a moment and nodded, 'Thank you, Sister, that means a lot to me.'

The gathering crowd looked up as the Elders lifted the veil of secrecy and prepared to disclose the outcome. The Eldest Brother cleared his throat and looked around the assembled Harper Bludlin Guild.

'Thank you, Brothers and Sisters, for attending this meeting. As you all know it is a very difficult decision to consent to one of our family members' rebirth, and the decision to do so is taken seriously. A thorough analysis of the situation is undertaken by all members of the Elders.' He rubbed his chin.

'Therefore with a heavy heart I call forth the following members of our Bludlin: Graadam, Ihishi-al, Ardaleigh and Tobias. You have all reached a point in your evolution that a rebirth is required to further aid your transition to the next level.'

The words hit Ardaleigh as though he was struck by a falling boulder. He dropped to his knees, defeated. Amberley placed her hand onto his shoulder and squeezed hard. He couldn't move. Tomace had won. His passionate words had left no lasting impact on the Guild, and he was to be lost to his twin flame for another life cycle.

'No—Starlah, I am sorry I have failed you,' he whispered, clutching his pendant.

The Eldest Brother descended off his throne and approached Ardaleigh. He stood before him with his hand extended to him. 'Please stand, Younger Brother. Do not see this as a failure. A rebirth is never cast in punishment; it is always a way to advance your soul.'

Ardaleigh lifted up his hand and allowed the Elder to help him to his feet. He felt drained and numb. What would she do without him? What trouble would she get herself into? He wouldn't know. He no longer would be able to watch over her or feel her presence. He squeezed his eyes shut, trying to squeeze out the truth.

'Katalin, please help our Young Bludlin to his chambers and help him prepare for the birthing process. Ardaleigh, you have until the second moon's appearance before you are summoned to the birthing chamber. I suggest you set your mind at peace,' the Eldest Brother said before turning to join the other gathered members. He approached the other three members about to be rebirthed and relayed the same message.

Katalin clutched Ardaleigh by the arm. He remained quiet as she guided him back to his chambers. He still couldn't believe that it was as simple as a few words spoken and his whole existence had changed. He had no idea who his parents would be, what type of life he would have and when, if ever, he would be in Starlah's arms again.

Once he was in the birthing chamber his new life would be disclosed to him. He would have the opportunity to reflect on the lessons he would be facing and how he was to evolve through this particular life. But in this moment the fear of what lay ahead pierced his heart.

The whole birthing process was not new to him, given his numerous lives through the Third Realm. It didn't make it any easier though. Each time it became more torturous being forced apart from his twin flame.

Some lives were easier than others, as the choice to be rebirthed, the type of family and life experience you wanted, and with whom, was yours. But when a rebirth was forced upon you, those elements were taken out of your control, and your life experience was a consequence of the combined deliberation of the Elders and what they deemed apt for your soul's betterment.

Ardaleigh had hoped that the both of them had evolved beyond the rebirthing process and that they both would ascend this next cycle. It seemed that wasn't to be. Once Ardaleigh commenced the next life through the Third Realm he would be propelled into three more life cycles before he would be up for ascension again.

Starlah's current life was her last before she was up for consideration for ascension, depending on whether she was able to transcend her lessons. He grabbed his shirt and squeezed it tight as though it was his heart that he was squeezing. If only he could squeeze out the pain.

Katalin opened the door to his chamber and guided him in. She closed the door and took him to his room. 'Brother, you know the routine. You must bathe and meditate prior to being summoned to the birthing chamber.'

She sat him on the bed and grabbed him by the shoulders. 'Ardaleigh, enough of this—it's time. Now go and bathe. I will leave you to do so and will return to meditate with you.'

He cringed. 'Very well. Leave me be, but do not return. I will meditate alone.'

'As you wish, Brother.' She turned to leave, stopped at the door and hesitated, 'Ardaleigh, I embrace your essence.' She looked saddened. 'I wish you joy in your new life.' She walked out and closed the door.

His heart pounded in his ears with anger, sadness and regret. He exhaled, surrendering to his fate, and went about doing what was required.

TWENTY-SEVEN

STARLAH STARED at her watch; it was 2:45 pm. She gathered her things, getting ready to leave to meet up with Bella. It would take her an hour to drive out to the Todd family's beach house and she didn't want to be late. Her palms felt damp and she had trouble keeping her mind focused on anything except what she was going to say to Bella.

She had reread the message a dozen times, and each time she had an uneasy feeling in the pit of her solar plexus. *Nerves,* she concluded. She grabbed her keys and left a brief note telling Daniel where she was going. She didn't want him to worry about her, not when he had his own problems to sort out. Her abdomen contracted into a tight ball. *Please keep him safe.*

She jumped into her car and turned the ignition. The car hummed. She sucked in a deep breath and shook her hands before putting the car into gear. *Right, let's go.* She pulled out of the driveway.

She cranked up the music hoping it would keep her distracted, but with each passing kilometre her palms got damper. She worried that by the time she arrived they would be dripping. Great, she thought, how was she supposed to greet Bella? She would flick her hands up into a 'hi' gesture and send waves of sweat all over her. She visualised the scene and shook her head at her own craziness.

She wiped her palms onto her jeans and blew on them to dry them. She drove until she saw the sign welcoming people to Kipper's Cove, and her heart quickened: fifteen minutes to go. She took a deep breath in and exhaled through pursed, dry lips.

She gave a nervous chuckle. Was there any reason to be nervous? It was, after all, just a visit with her friend. It wasn't like Bella would try to kill her or anything—right? No, of course not, stupid, she shook her head—just another innocent visit. That's all.

She turned off into Beach Avenue, the street leading down to the Todd's beach house, remembering she had to turn off into the dirt road, through the dense coastal she-oak and banksia. When she hit the row of beach spinifex she knew she had arrived. She released her tight grip around the steering wheel and slumped in the seat.

'Show time,' she told the empty car. She turned the ignition off and stared at the double-storey white weatherboard house.

She closed her eyes and pictured last year's Christmas break there. Bella's parents made her feel so welcome, and for the first time in her life she felt like she had belonged. She felt her throat tighten. She missed that.

She opened her eyes and tried to swallow the lump bulging in her throat. She hoped with all her heart that Bella would welcome her back but then she remembered why she was here. How was she ever to have a friendship with Bella and her family when Brad came with that package? She couldn't and that broke her heart.

With time she would get over what Brad did to her, but she would feel Bella's absence always. She swallowed the lump down and pulled her shoulders back. She opened the car door and stepped outside. She looked down at her wrist and checked the time: 3:44 pm. Good, she wasn't late.

She flicked her eyes around the place. There wasn't any evidence that Bella was here yet, so she made her way up the driveway to the front door to wait. Her feet crunched across the gravel pathway. She felt out of place amongst the deserted vegetation and structure of the beach house as though she was intruding upon the solitude with her awkward steps.

She climbed the steps leading to the front door and noticed a note stuck to the front door.

Hey Starlah, let yourself in. I've just gone to get some munchies. Won't be long.

She pulled it off the door and examined it. For some weird reason Bella had typed the letter instead of scribbling it on a piece of paper. It was like she had pre-planned being out.

She shrugged and opened the door. She walked through the hallway and into the spacious living room filled with blue and green beachy décor. There was a massive white leather lounge taking up most of the room, facing a fifty inch LED TV with an impressive sound system. She remembered it well from watching a horror movie at full throttle. Scared the hell out of her.

She felt the hairs at the back of her neck stand to attention. She scrunched her shoulders up and down a few times, trying to shake out the weird feeling rocking her body. She clutched her keys and handbag close to her body; something wasn't right. She darted her eyes around the room and called out, 'Bella, you here?'

No answer came. She hesitated in the hallway and turned her head to look back at the front door. It responded by opening. Her heart jumped. She opened her eyes wide, holding her breath—*Please be Bella—please be Bella.*

It creaked, opening in slow motion to reveal its guest. 'Oh, it's you,' she stammered.

'Hello Starlah, sorry Bella couldn't make it. I hated the idea of you being here all alone, so here I am.' He waved his hand in front of him, grinning.

Her body quivered. 'Brad …'

He stepped through the door and turned to lock it with the key, so there was no way she could open it. He put the keys into his shorts pocket and smirked as though daring her to come and get them. He walked past her into the living room.

'Come in, make yourself at home. I'll go get us some drinks.' He turned his head to look over his shoulder and winked at her as he went into the kitchen.

She didn't move—no, not again. She darted her eyes around

the beach house trying to remember its layout. There was a sliding door out back that opened up into the backyard which faced the beach. It was locked with a key, which she supposed he had on him. Shit.

She scanned her eyes over the windows. The numerous ceiling-to-floor windows were all protected by security screens. Her heart sank as she realised there was no escape route. She would have to get the front door keys. She winced. How the hell was she going to accomplish that when they were in his pocket?

He whistled as he gathered the glasses and alcohol from the cabinets. She could hear him open the fridge to get some ice out. The ice chinked as it dropped into the glass, sending a shiver throughout her body.

He came back out into the living room holding two glasses filled with scotch. 'Oh babes, you look freaked out. Come over here and relax with a drink. It's gonna be a long night, might as well enjoy.' He walked over to the solid wood mahogany coffee table, put down the two glasses and looked up at her.

She clutched her pendant, expecting it to be heated up by Ardaleigh's presence. It remained cold. Where was he? She fought back the tears. 'Brad, what the hell's going on? Where's Bella? Why isn't she here? Why didn't she text me to say she couldn't come?'

'Well, because she doesn't know anything about it. That's why. I wrote that text using her phone. Pretty clever, hey?' He walked over and stood in front of her. 'I needed to see you to make things right between us, and I knew that you wouldn't come if you knew it was me.'

She pulled her shoulders back. 'I'm not interested in anything you have to say. I trusted you once, and I won't make that mistake again.' She held down the venom wanting to boil forth. Better not antagonise him too much, she warned herself.

'Oh Starlah, feisty as ever. You really do make me laugh,' he grinned as though she made a joke. 'Now come and sit down,' he ordered.

She wiped her hand across her mouth. She darted her eyes around as though somehow an escape route would jump up and wave its hands at her saying, 'This way'. She swallowed hard, walked over to where he was pointing and took a seat on the spacious lounge. She hoped that he would sit on the other end.

He didn't; he came around, took a seat next to her and exhaled loudly. 'Now this is cosy, hey?' He made a pretence of looking around the layout of the beach house and smiled. 'Remember last Christmas? We had such a great time, didn't we?'

He turned to look at her face. 'I remember that night. We were left alone after everyone went to bed, and we talked for an hour. That's when I knew we had something special.' He leaned over and clutched her hand, which felt hot against her cold skin. 'You felt it too, right?' He looked into her eyes with hope then shook his head. 'That's why I'm confused.' He let go of her hand, grabbed his drink and took a sip, swallowing noisily.

She stared at him, mouth gaping. What fuckin' planet was he on? What she remembered was them spending like ten minutes talking about the movie they just watched, and she excused herself as soon as there was a break in the conversation. His wounded *Dear John* look pissed her off.

'Why won't you give me a chance, Starlah?' He spun his head around to face her again. 'What don't I have? Whatever it is I'll get it.' He pouted his lips. He reminded her of Bella.

'Brad, you and I … we can't ever be.' She tilted her head and frowned. 'You tried to rape me. On what planet do you reckon I would be OK with that?' She shook her head and looked away.

His face contorted. 'That was your fault. You can't tease a bloke and not expect him to think he was gonna get a bit. Fuck.' He jumped to his feet and paced around.

She recognised the rabid animal and clutched her throat. 'Sorry …' Rising, she went over to him and grabbed his hand. 'I was confused and scared. Please calm down. Let's talk about it.' She led him back to the lounge and sat down.

He sat down next to her and looked imploringly into her eyes. She would have felt sorry for him if it wasn't for the fact he was a delusional, unpredictable lunatic. 'OK—um, I'm sorry that things got out of control. I didn't mean to make you angry, but I could never betray my friendship with Bella.' She tried to appease the devoted brother she knew was in him.

He contemplated what she was saying, nodding. After a few head nods he smirked. 'Nice try, Starlah.'

She cringed. It wasn't going to be that easy to appease him.

'You see, Bella would never have had to know about it.' He leaned over so his face was inches away from her shoulder. Her shoulders were exposed. *Damn it,* she should have worn a leather jacket with sharp pointy studs on it. He lingered as though he was going to take a chunk out of her. She monitored his mouth, waiting for him to bare his teeth.

He softly kissed her shoulder. 'See, the world won't end because she doesn't know about this.'

She pulled back and quivered. She closed her eyes and wished he would wake up from this delusion of them ever being together. 'Stop,' she ordered him. 'Please just stop this.'

He laughed and sat back. 'Whatever.' He picked up his glass and took another swig. 'Ah—love this scotch, you should have some.'

ARDALEIGH STOOD in the bathing cubicle and allowed the ultrasonic waves to cleanse his body. He hoped that it would also cleanse his mind. The chamber switched off. He stepped out and pulled his shoulders back, taking in a deep crisp breath. He felt lightened. Bathing was the first step in the cleansing process. It was more symbolic than physical.

Gathering his white silky gown, he pulled it over his head and allowed the material to flow down his body. Physically he was ready. Now he had to get his mind in order.

He walked over to the corner of the room and stood in front of the clear quartz crystal, which was the size of a soccer ball, and stared at its iridescent glow. It welcomed him. He felt the draw from the crystal, and he sat down on the large purple and silver embossed cushion and readied himself for the meditation process. He tried to push the image of Starlah out of his brain, but it was a difficult task. She kept floating through his mind, reminding him of all the things he would be missing.

He focused his mind and energy onto the base of his spine and breathed in, drawing in the energy from the crystal, and directed it up his spine to the top of his head. He visualised the purple light exploding out of the top of his crown and floating upwards. It felt exhilarating. His body responded and completely relaxed.

He continued to focus his mind on the gentle pulsing light cascading through his body and allowed the vibrating energy to dispel the heartache and pain from his body and mind. He surrendered to the process.

He pressed the tip of his tongue to the roof of his mouth and continued to draw and circulate the energy through his body. He felt the energy coiling and contracting, then expanding through his body, unwinding and transcending as it ascended up his spine.

The intensity continued to build through his body until it crescendoed and exploded out the top of his crown, momentarily causing him to lose all his senses. He sat in that space for a while, allowing the silence to soothe his being.

He felt lighter. The process was complete. He surrendered to his soul's needs. He let his eyes flutter open.

'I am pleased to see the peace on your face, Brother.' Katalin announced her presence. She sat behind him in mediation pose.

Ardaleigh smiled. 'Sister Katalin, I see you have forgotten my request.' He got to his feet and walked over to her.

'Yes, my memory is not what it used to be, my apologies.'

Smiling, she gracefully got to her feet and touched him on his shoulder. 'I will always be here for you Ardaleigh, even if you think I am against you.'

'Thank you for not giving up on me.' He looked down to the floor and sighed. 'I accept the need for a rebirth, and I hope I do not fail to transcend my inability to remain balanced in love.'

'That is one of the hardest things to overcome, Brother, not to lose oneself while loving another.' She leaned into him and placed her forehead against his. 'I embrace your essence.'

He closed his eyes and whispered, 'As do I yours.'

They heard the summoning horn declaring the ascension of the second moon and the time for him to make his way to the birthing chamber. He swallowed hard. 'Could you please escort me to the birthing chamber?'

She looked compassionately into his eyes. 'Of course, Brother.'

BRAD SCULLED the remaining scotch in the glass and crunched on the ice. 'So what should we do? Do you want to watch a DVD?' He looked at her as though he was asking a friend a casual question. Nowhere in his face did it register that what he was doing was wrong.

Starlah darted her eyes around, continuing to assess the potential for escape. 'Um, sure ... but nothing scary.' She couldn't cope with watching horror as well as living it.

'OK, let's see what we've got.' He walked over to the extensive DVD cabinet and fingered through the DVDs. He pulled out two and showed them to her. 'How about one of these?'

She eyed the two cases and pointed to the one in his left hand. 'That one looks good.' She had already watched it and knew it was a light comedy.

'Cool,'—he smiled—'see, we can do this.' He put the DVD

in and went into the kitchen to top up his drink. 'Do you want something? If scotch ain't your thing then we have lots of other flavours. Wine? Beer?'

She swallowed and her mouth felt dry, so she answered, 'A Coke would be good if you have it.' She shook her head. She was trying to act as though this was a normal situation, and it was doing her head in. Her heart continued to pound, making her feel short of breath and jittery.

He grabbed a can of Coke and dropped some ice into a tall glass. Opening the pantry he pulled out a bag of un-popped popcorn and put it into the microwave. Smiling he watched it spin and pop. He looked relaxed and like the Brad she knew as Bella's brother, but under the façade she knew the rabid animal crouched, waiting for its opportunity to pounce.

'Here we go …' He put her drink down next to her on the coffee table and placed the bowl of popcorn in the middle.

She reached over, grabbed the glass and swallowed a few mouthfuls, hoping it would relieve the desert in her mouth. She eyed him up and down. He looked casual in his khaki camouflage shorts and dark green T-shirt. He had his hair slicked back with product, and he was cleanly shaven, as though this really was a date.

She grabbed her pendant, hoping it would transfer courage to her. It remained lifeless. She felt the panic rising. *Ardaleigh … where are you?* She pleaded through her mind. No answer came. Tears burned her eyes. She turned to watch the TV, hoping Brad wouldn't see.

Moving closer to her he grabbed the bowl of popcorn and

shoved it into her face. 'Here, have some,' he said as though it was an order, not merely an offer.

She reached her hand out, grabbed a few pieces and raised them to her lips. She had trouble aiming for her mouth with her trembling fingers and dropped more than she managed to put into her mouth. 'Thanks.'

He leaned back onto the couch and smiled. He grabbed a large handful and shoved them into his mouth, dropping a few himself. He looked content, chewing away, laughing at the movie.

She closed her eyes and wished he would choke on the popcorn.

And then he did. He coughed and splattered, pounding his chest. He coughed out, 'Pass me my drink.'

She looked at his drink and thought about throwing it into his face and running. She picked it up and brought it towards him.

He clicked his fingers, hurrying her up.

Her hand shook, and she dropped the glass onto his lap.

He jumped up still coughing and glared at her. 'You idiot, now look at what you've done.' He managed to croak out.

She cringed. 'Sorry.' She jumped up onto her feet as well, getting ready to defend herself.

He walked away into the kitchen, swearing in between bouts of coughing, stepping out of sight.

Starlah looked around. *Please, please show me a way out.* She eyed off the stairs and felt her spine tingle. *That way.* She checked that he was still out of sight, grabbed her bag and keys and made a run for the stairs. Maybe she could climb out the window from one of the bedrooms upstairs. They shouldn't be as secure as the downstairs ones.

She raced up the stairs as unobtrusively as she could. She was almost to the top when she heard him call out to her.

'Hey, sorry about going off. I was just …'

She froze.

'Starlah, where are you?' he sang out. 'Don't try and hide from me, coz you know you can't. I'll find you, and when I do I won't be very happy.'

Dashing into his parents' bedroom she hurried to the window and tried to yank it open. It was locked. 'Shit.' She ran out of that bedroom and towards Bella's room.

He thundered up the stairs towards her. 'Oh, there you are …' He gritted his teeth, 'I thought you had disappeared on me.' He wiped his hand across his forehead. 'Wouldn't want that now, would we?' He grabbed her arm and yanked her towards him. 'Now come here.'

She winced and flew in the direction he pulled. 'I was just going to the toilet, please let go.' She held back tears.

His neck veins bulged. 'So what was wrong with the toilet downstairs then?' he said between gritted teeth.

She pulled her arm free and rubbed it. 'I forgot where that one was, OK? Jeez, give me a break will you?'

A smile crept across his face; how she would love to smash that smirk right off his psycho face. She clenched her fists.

'Oh OK, no probs then. I just assumed you were doing a runner. My bad.' He rubbed the corner of his bottom lip. He tilted his head as he face changed. He leaned in closer. 'Just as well, or there would be a problem.'

And there it was; the rabid animal was back. The hairs on the back of her neck and arms jumped to attention. Her whole body buzzed in flight/fright mode.

ARDALEIGH TRIED to keep his mind off the reality that he wouldn't be able to see, feel or even remember Starlah, and he focused on what was required of him. He nodded and smiled politely as Katalin talked. She had her arm looped through his, guiding him towards his programmed chamber. His heart quickened as they approached. He noted the crowd gathering and his heart sank.

The crystal dome-shaped pods, resembling igloos, illuminated the surrounding area, welcoming the four members to be rebirthed. Each pod was programmed and fixed for a certain family in the Third Realm.

He hoped his new parents would be loving and kind. His transgression surely didn't warrant parents like Starlah's. He prayed not. What would they name him? He closed his eyes, and hoped they would call him by his true name.

He had hope; if Starlah's drunken parents could pick up on her name frequency, then his awaiting parents might also. He sighed, knowing that was unlikely, given most rebirths resulted in unfamiliar naming. He would have to embrace whatever they named him. Maybe they would go with 'Simon'; he wouldn't mind being named that again.

'Welcome, Brothers and Sisters. It is time to send off some of our own to live lives in an embodied realm. Please take this time to say goodbye and send forth prayers of love.' The Eldest Brother folded his hands in front of him and commenced a silent prayer.

The other members mimicked their Elder. There was a hushed murmur rippling around the gathered Harper Guild. The energy was palpable. Normally Ardaleigh would have welcomed the feeling, but not today. Not when it was his journey they were praying for.

'Thank you once again. Now please step forward, Graadam, Ihishi-al, Ardaleigh and Tobias. Make your way to your assigned chambers, and enter.' The Eldest Brother commanded.

The four of them turned and embraced their guides. Katalin gazed into Ardaleigh's eyes and smiled with warmth and affection. She hugged him hard and whispered, 'Take the path to the right, Brother. It will lead to a very happy existence.' She pulled away and cast her eyes down.

Ardaleigh frowned. He opened his mouth to ask what she meant by that but was whisked away and led to his chamber by the birthing Elder. He turned and looked over his shoulder at Katalin one last time and smiled. 'I embrace your essence, Katalin.'

She clutched her hand against her heart. 'As do I yours, Ardaleigh.' She nodded in encouragement.

He had to bend down to enter the chamber. He went and sat in the reclining chair, tilting back so he could face the big dome screen above that would highlight and reveal his life ahead to him. The door closed and sealed him in. Once the birthing process commenced there was no way to stop it.

The chamber hummed, increasing in intensity and frequency. The surrounding crystals pulsed around him, infusing his body with oscillating energy. The birthing process had been initiated. He would spend the next few hours increasing his vibration to purify his being, and then he would decrease it to be re-embodied.

Once his body reached a certain frequency he would be teleported through the bridge and then enter the foetus of the chosen family as it descended through the birthing canal of his mother to be. He would be greeted into his new life, without any memories of his previous lives.

THIRTY-ONE

STARLAH'S HEART continued to pound in her ears. Her throat felt raw. She manoeuvred the keys in her hands so the car key poked through her clenched fingers in case she needed to punch him in the face with it. This time she would do him harm if she had to.

'Why did you have to ruin it? I was enjoying our time together.' He rubbed his mouth, like he did that night. 'Fuck, Starlah!' He looked as though he was going to cry.

She didn't have it in her to placate him anymore so she remained quiet.

'Answer me,' he yelled.

She jumped and clutched her throat. 'Um, sorry …' was all she could get out.

He paced in front of her. 'Seriously, I don't get you—I do everything to make you feel at home, and this is the thanks I get.' He glared at her. 'When will you learn to stop being such a frigid bitch?' He clenched his jaw.

She pulled her handbag close to her chest and clutched the keys. They dug into her skin. She looked past him towards Bella's room. God, she hoped the window would be open in there. She inched her way around him so she had her back towards Bella's room and he was facing the stairs. Her fingers itched. This might be her only opportunity to immobilise him.

He darted his head towards her. 'What the fuck do you think you're doing?'

'Nothing,' she gulped.

Leaping towards her he grabbed her shoulders and pulled her into his body. She dropped her bag and keys. She could smell the scotch on his breath. God only knew how many he had before she arrived. They were standing at the top of the stairs. He turned her so she was the one that was standing over the edge of the stairs.

She closed her eyes, expecting him to push her down. He pushed her away from his body threatening to do so. 'Please Brad, don't do this.'

He shook his head. 'I should just end this. I'm sick of this game.' He tormented her by pushing her further out, so she now had to try to counterbalance her body by leaning towards him. She opened her eyes and stared up at the ceiling. She could feel her back tingle in preparation for impact.

'I loved you, Starlah, but if you don't want me then I couldn't stand to see you with anyone else.' He gripped tighter around her upper arms and pushed the top of her body back so she was arched over the stairs backwards. Her hair dangled over the edge as gravity taunted her.

She gritted her teeth. He was being such a clichéd psycho. She was sure she had heard that line in a movie before. Loved her—as if he would even know what that meant. She closed her eyes again. She resigned herself to her fate. She swallowed hard and braced herself.

Daniel flashed through her mind. She hoped that he would be OK after she was gone. *He'd better keep his promise about getting away from Davo,* she thought. Davo – she wanted to feel anger towards him for getting her brother into his messed-up situation, but there was something about him that seemed good.

She saw a flash of Sara and hoped she would be there for Daniel. Would they get married and have kids together? That made her smile – Danny as a dad … totally wild.

Her mind drifted towards Ardaleigh. She felt her heart tremble at the thought of finally returning to him. She smiled. *I'm coming home, my love.*

'Why the hell are you smiling?' Brad yelled into her face.

She could no longer hear him. Her mind detached and took her home—she was happy. She pictured Ardaleigh's smile. She expected him to be there to greet her. Why wasn't he here with her now? What if something had happened? No, she would not believe that. She would hold onto the fact he would be there to greet her.

Brad shook her; nothing … she continued to smile. He let go of one shoulder and slapped her hard across the face. She dangled over the stairs.

She felt that. She blinked a few times and reorientated to her surroundings. 'No. Let me go home.' She looked into Brad's tormented face and screamed.

The front door busted open, sending chunks of wood from the doorframe into the air. It sounded as though a car was crashing through the door. They both jumped. Brad pulled Starlah back towards him and stared hard at the door.

A large figure burst through the door and yelled. 'Oi crazy, let her go man. Nice and gentle.' He dropped the ramming rod and grabbed his gun.

Who was it? Starlah continued to stare in a daze at the authoritative figure below. The gun looked threatening and real. He looked familiar.

'Are you OK, Starlah?' he asked, continuing to hold the gun pointed at Brad.

Brad pulled Starlah across his body, using her as a shield. 'Who the hell are you? What are you doing in my house? You're trespassing, you know.' Brad glared down at the threatening figure.

She could tell Brad was freaked out. His body trembled. It was the first time she saw any glimpse of fear in him.

'I'm Detective Sergeant Dave Lewis. Let her go, Brad. It ain't worth it.' He moved closer to the stairs without taking his eyes or gun off Brad.

Finally it hit Starlah—it was Davo, Daniel's Davo. What the hell? That made no sense. 'Dave, what's going on? Where's Daniel? Is he all right?'

Dave chuckled. 'Danny told me you always thought about

others above yourself. Yeah, all's good with Danny boy. He sent me here for you. He thought you might be in trouble. Good senses, that one.' He gripped the gun tighter. 'So Brad, how about it? You gonna let her go, or do I have to put a bullet in the middle of your fuckin' forehead?'

Brad jittered from one foot to the other behind her. He clutched her tight. 'Get the hell out of my house. This is between me and Starlah.' His faced burned with rage.

'Nah, ain't gonna happen, bro. There's only one way I'm leaving here, and that's with her.' Dave took another tentative step towards the stairs.

Brad gritted his teeth. 'Fine, have her,' he spat, pushing her hard over the edge of the stairs and running towards his room.

Everything slowed down. Starlah had some awareness she was falling, but it didn't register fully. She felt removed from the event. It was as though she was watching a movie with her as the guest star.

She tumbled hard. First, she snapped her wrist, as she extended her arm out automatically to brace herself against the fall. A loud popping sound echoed around the room, and she screamed out, more in shock than pain.

She continued to somersault down the stairs, hitting her shoulder then the side of her head. Finally her back came crashing down onto the floor. Her head snapped backwards with a sickening whack against the tiled floor.

'Oh fuck! Starlah, you OK?' Dave ran to her. He yelled into his two-way, asking for an ambo and backup.

She wanted to answer him and say she was OK, but her brain

seemed to have forgotten how to make her mouth work. Instead she decided to allow herself to drift off into the darkness, where hopefully Ardaleigh was waiting.

Instead of Ardaleigh's beautiful smile she was greeted by Jacob. 'Hello, sister.' He smiled, not with malice though, which confused her.

'What are you doing here, Jacob?' She still had enough sense to know that he didn't fit into this scene. He did remind her of someone though. She searched her brain, and then it hit her—Brad. That's who he resembled. She shivered in recognition. 'What's going on, Jacob? None of this is making any sense.'

He looked at her with compassion. 'Sometimes the one that brings us the deepest heartache and trauma is the one that brings us closest to the truth.'

'What–' she stammered through her chattering teeth. It was getting colder, and she had to concentrate on his words to remain focused. They felt important.

'Starlah, Brad wasn't sent in punishment to you. He was a gift to help you transcend your guilt and shame over what happened between us.' He glowed.

'Brad is an extension of my essence, and the Elders implored my participation to help you become enlightened so you may ascend. The moment has arrived for you to transcend this life journey's core lesson. If you fail I am afraid that reunion with your Bludlin will no longer be possible. You will be expelled and must merge with another guild. Then you'll restart your life in a different dimension without your twin flame.'

'Please Starlah, this is your fourth life since our time together, and you are yet to embrace the truth.' He reached out. 'I do not want our life together to be the reason you lose everything.'

A deep pain pieced her heart and shook it to its core. It throbbed and clawed through the chambers, seeking out the truth hidden in there. It demanded unveiling: *What do you want me to know?* She wanted to scream.

'Jacob please, please forgive me. My soul bleeds with the knowledge that my hands ended your life.' She sobbed from the depths of her being. 'But I don't know what I must do to make amends.'

He edged closer, and she felt his love wash over her. 'Forgiveness *is* the key, but it's not my forgiveness you need to seek.' He smiled. 'That you already have.'

'Well then, tell me. Whose forgiveness do I need to get? Tell me, and I'll beg for it, now.' She trembled violently.

'It is not my soul that seeks illumination. It is your soul that has bled with the pain of your actions. It is your soul that is demanding enlightenment. Heed its call, Starlah.'

He extended his arm, welcoming a vibrant bright light. It appeared before her in the shape of an orb. It pulsed and inched its way closer. Starlah's initial response was to run away and hide, but there was something soothing and kind about the energy of the light that she couldn't resist and she continued to stare into its effervescent glow.

Her body floated up and faced the light. It shimmered. 'Do you embrace me?'

Starlah didn't hesitate. 'Yes. I do.'

Contracting into a small sphere the light gravitated towards her cupped, outstretched hands and landed on her palms. Its warmth was all-encompassing. 'If you embrace me, then bring me into your heart, and ask the person whose forgiveness you need to seek.'

Starlah sealed her hands around the pulsing orb and brought it to her heart. A rush of pure, intense energy surged through her heart and exploded through her body. She dropped to her knees sobbing. It was right there in front of her the whole time. The one person whose forgiveness she thought never mattered enough to ask for.

'Do you see it now, sister?' Jacob placed his hand upon her shoulder and sent loving waves of energy through her.

Starlah continued to sob, nodding. 'Yes.'

'Well then, ask for it and be free.'

She clutched herself and rocked back and forth, and the pain deep within seeped out through every pore. It released its toxic effects from her body, evaporated into a golden mist and transcended upwards. Her lips trembled as she whispered to herself, 'Please forgive me.'

The orb of her soul exploded and seared forgiveness throughout her whole body and soul. She was finally united. She collapsed onto the floor. The truth resonated through her heart and dispersed the veil clouding her consciousness. She felt like screaming it from the top of the world. She couldn't wait to tell Ardaleigh that she was able to embrace self-forgiveness. Now they both could ascend and remain together always. No more rebirths, no more having to spend lifetimes apart. As the liberation of truth soothed her like a healing balm she exhaled a long, deep breath. *Ardaleigh, my love, I'm coming home.*

THIRTY-TWO

ARDALEIGH BRACED himself as the birthing chamber prepared him for his new life. Physical sensations rocked his body. The purification process was known to be painful. He took a deep breath and accepted the transformation.

The scattered holographic image above him refocused to reveal a clear image. He saw his family-to-be. His mother rubbed her belly, singing a lullaby to the baby inside her. She glowed with love and joy. He was going to be a loved and a wanted child – relief washed over him.

He saw an image of his father-to-be at work, completely engrossed in what he was doing, and intuitively knew he would be an absent father. He felt saddened by that.

The screen reshuffled, and another image appeared. His birth would be a difficult and painful one, with his mother dying during the birthing process. Tears washed down his face.

He wiped at his tears, nodding. He understood why that would happen: he would learn to love without attachments by loving her in absence.

Throughout his life he would face difficult and tempting challenges as a way to cope with the loss of his mother, but he hoped that he would make the right decisions. He hoped that his guide would have an easier time getting through to him than he did with Starlah.

He smiled, taking in her memory one last time before she would disappear from his consciousness. He whispered, 'I love you, Starlah,' closed his eyes and sent his love to her. He hoped that wherever she was she would feel it.

The chamber let off a high-pitched pulse; the contractions had commenced. His body vibrated with such force his molecules scattered and rose through the ceiling and into the teleporting tunnel, bridging the two realms. A kaleidoscope of colours zoomed towards him. He jolted this way and that through the birthing tunnel. His heart raced, but his mind remained pure.

He closed his eyes and sent silent prayers to Starlah, wishing her an amazing safe life without him. He prayed that she would forgive him for leaving her again.

He came to a sudden stop. He blinked several times, focusing hard on the two illuminated paths in front of him, beckoning to him. Katalin's words echoed through his mind: *Take the path on the right. It will lead to a very happy existence.*

He didn't know where this path would take him or how

she had managed to manipulate the birthing process, but he trusted her and focused his energy on the path on the right and recommenced the journey. A bright light exploded before him, signalling his arrival.

'STARLAH. STARLAH, can you hear me?' A voice called to her from the fog.

Ardaleigh, is that you? She tried to call back.

'I don't know if she can hear me. God, please wake up … it's me, Daniel.' He squeezed her hand.

She struggled to open her eyes, but they felt glued shut. Her throat felt full as though something was shoved in there causing her to want to gag, but she couldn't remember how. She felt as though she was a disembodied mind. If only she could make her voice work so the person holding her hand would know she was OK. But was she OK? She wasn't sure.

'I'm so sorry, Danny boy. I'm sorry I couldn't stop her from getting hurt. I thought I was getting through to him, but that scumbag really is a psycho. Just glad we got him locked up.'

She heard a male voice say. 'He'll be put away for attempted murder. That's like twenty-five years, bro.'

'Yeah, just as well or I'd be locked up for fuckin' smashing the bastard's skull in.'

She desperately wanted to reach out to him, to soothe his pain. Why couldn't she freaking move? *Aargh, move, useless arms—please just a little bit.*

'Quick, get the nurse. I felt her hand squeeze mine. I'm sure of it,' yelled the voice above her.

'Quick, get the doctor. I think he's waking up,' the nurse called out to her colleague.

His eyes fluttered open and he was blinded by bright light. He snapped them shut again. He felt heavy and disorientated; where the hell was he? He tentatively opened one eye and squinted. 'Where am I?' he croaked.

The nurse came around to his side and clasped his hand. 'You're in hospital. You were in an accident.' She cleared her throat. 'We thought we had lost you.'

He blinked his eyes. They still felt heavy. 'Lost me where?' He squinted up into her eyes.

She laughed. 'No, I meant that'—she hesitated then continued—'we thought you had um, well, died basically.' She continued to smile. 'You scared the hell out of us—glad you made it back to us.'

'Died. Whoa, really?' He couldn't believe what she was

saying. He didn't have any memories of what she was talking about.

'Yeah, they brought you in last night after you were hit by a car on your bike.' She wiped his blond fringe out of his eyes. 'Can you remember anything? Do you know what your name is?' She smiled compassionately.

'Um, my name—Ard?' He couldn't remember.

'Art? Is that as in Arthur?' she queried.

He wasn't sure, but he answered, 'Yeah.' He turned his head and scanned over the hospital décor. There was a picture of a snow-capped mountain on the bare wall, and a TV hung down from the ceiling facing his bed. He looked at the side table, noticed a bunch of flowers sitting in a vase and wondered who had given them to him.

'Are they from my family?' He nodded in their direction.

She walked over to them and fingered through the pink and white carnations. 'No, they were left over from a discharged patient, and I thought they were too beautiful to throw out. Since we didn't know who you were or if you had any family I thought you would like them. I snuck them in past my boss— shh.' She put her finger across her mouth and smiled. She picked them up and held them in front of him. 'Do you like them?'

He simply stared at them.

'So Arthur, do you have a surname?' She put the flowers back down.

He didn't know so he darted his eyes around the room and focused on the picture on the wall. 'Snow,' he answered.

'OK, now we're getting somewhere, Mr Arthur Snow.' She came back around to his side and moved his hair out of his eyes again. 'Nice to meet you.'

236

MR ROSE, I'm sorry but I can't see any change in her condition. It may have been a spasm,' said a female voice in the distance.

'No! She definitely squeezed my hand. Take another look,' ordered the male, holding her hand. His hand felt warm and comforting.

'Very well,' said the female voice. She sighed and proceeded to pull back Starlah's eyelids and flash a pen-torch into her eyes. 'Mm … there's definitely more of a pupil response. That's good. But it's still one day at a time, Mr Rose.' She spoke with empathy.

'I knew it,' whispered the male voice. 'I knew she could hear me.' His voice cracked, and he squeezed her hand even tighter.

Arthur tried to sit up in bed, but his body felt as though it belonged to someone else. The doctor and nurses finished their assessment of him and left shaking their heads in disbelief. He didn't know what the big deal was anyway. They reckoned he was knocked around pretty bad and died, and now he was doing great. He didn't feel great.

They had no reason to lie to him, but none of it made any sense. He picked up the bed controller and elevated the bed. He could see the friendly nurse out by the desk, talking animatedly with her colleagues. They giggled and pointed to one of the handsome doctors in the corridor. Arthur smiled.

He looked back over at the flowers and wondered why no one was here for him. Maybe he didn't have anyone. He wasn't sure. He pulled back the sheets and looked down at his body. He didn't recognise the body he was looking at.

His legs were bruised and grazed, but what surprised him the most was the thick layer of blond hair coating them. Somehow he thought he would have had dark hair, which would've have made more sense to him.

He concentrated on raising one leg then the other. They felt heavy and foreign. Maybe it was the head injury he sustained that was causing him to feel so removed from his body. He ran his fingers through his hair until he felt the large lump on the side of his skull. He pressed into it and winced. He cradled his head for a few seconds then took a deep breath.

He wanted to get out of bed and stretch his legs, but the bedrails were in the way. He grabbed the bedrail and shook it. Then he noticed the red latch down the side and pulled it in, dropping the rail. He swung one leg over the edge of the bed and then gradually the other. He sat there for a few moments, letting the blood circulate to the bottom of his feet. They tingled.

He pumped his legs up and down a few times until he thought he had the swing of things, then pushed himself over the edge of the bed and placed both feet on the cold linoleum floor.

A sharp pain travelled up his left leg, and he winced. Gritting his teeth he took a deep breath in and forced himself to stand. His leg gave way and he crumpled to the floor, hitting his hip against the floor. 'That did not feel too good,' he said between gritted teeth. He concentrated on taking slow deep breaths in and out until the pain subsided.

Once he had the pain under control he tried to use the bed to help him stand, and after a few more failed attempts he managed to get himself upright again. The pain in his leg was bearable this time, so he stood for a few minutes getting used to being upright. It felt good despite the throbbing pain.

When he thought it was safe to move he took a tentative step away from the bed, steadying himself by having his arms out to the sides as though balancing on a tightrope. It worked. He managed to take several steps without falling again.

He stumbled over to the sink and grabbed the sides, leaning onto it, huffing. He caught a glimpse of someone in the mirror. Shit, who the hell's that wreck? *Oh …*

He let go of one of the sides of the sink and brought his hand up to his face. He traced his index finger across the side of his jaw, turning his head. His pale green eyes stared at him dumbfounded. His shaggy dirty blond hair was matted and caked with blood, but it too didn't stir any recognition in him. His nose was swollen and crusted with old blood, but he doubted it would look familiar. As far as he was concerned he had woken up in someone else's body.

'What are you doing, Arthur? You aren't supposed to be out of bed yet,' the nurse chastised. 'Come on, let me help you back into bed. Can't have you stumbling around on your own. You might fall or something. Then I'll be in trouble.'

She placed her hand around the top of his arm and helped him walk back to his bed. Then she helped him swing his legs back into it. 'Now that's better, safe and sound.' She smiled at him. 'Next time you feel the need to go for a hike press on this, and I'll come with you. Got it?' She held up the nurse's call button.

'Yeah sorry.' He smiled back at her. 'Will do,' he assured.

THIRTY-FIVE

'No DANNY, don't leave me. Don't leave me here all by myself. Please. I can't stay here without you,' she pleaded, but he'd already gone. She clutched the pink teddy close to her.

A horrible pain burned inside her chest. She didn't know what it was, but she didn't have time to think about that. What should she do? Run after him? Yes, maybe he would take her with him. She had to pack her bag fast.

Jumping out of bed she grabbed her pink Barbie backpack, shoved in a handful of socks and picked up a dirty T-shirt from the floor. She didn't have time to find a clean one. It didn't matter anyway; Danny would wash it for her. She then grabbed her brush and–and–and what else would she need?

Nothing, just go, she told herself. She tiptoed towards Danny's room. It was empty. Her heart raced and the horrible feeling in her chest was getting bigger. She darted her eyes towards her parents' room and could hear them both snoring.

Tears pooled and spilled over her lids, but she gritted her teeth. She clutched the teddy and backpack close to her chest and continued to tiptoe to the front door. Maybe he was waiting there for her.

She turned the doorknob and it opened. See, he must have left it open for her. She smiled. She stepped out into the cold night air and stood there in her tattered nightie, waiting for him to jump out of the bushes and grab her by the hand and run. Run away from them and not look back.

She waited, and waited, holding her teddy tight, but he never came. She trembled, not just from the cold. She dropped her bag, hugged the teddy with both arms and stared out into the darkness calling out to him in a whisper.

She dropped to her knees, curled up and cried silently. She didn't want to wake her parents because he would come; she was sure of it. He'd never leave her like that. He'd never break her heart like that. She just had to be quiet and wait patiently.

She whispered, 'Please Danny, come back … please Danny, come back,' because she knew he would somehow be able to hear her. He was always pretty good at knowing when she needed him, and she needed him now. *Please Danny, come back …*

But her stupid eyes couldn't stay open anymore, and she eventually fell asleep chanting that over and over again.

She felt a kick to the side of her ribs.

❧

'Oh good morning, Mr Rose, we're just finishing up with Starlah's wash. We won't be long, if you wouldn't mind waiting outside for a few minutes?' a female voice was talking above her.

Things were getting closer. She felt as though more of her body was waking up. She felt the nurses washing her body and rolling her from side to side. Totally humiliating, but the fact she felt humiliation was a good thing.

She could also feel the annoying sting of the catheter in her bladder, the pressure of the bed under her shoulder blades and the comforting warmth of her brother's hand. *Her brother's hand.* She was relieved that she finally remembered who that hand belonged to.

That was the most rewarding thing for her, that she could remember Danny and what he meant to her. She recalled Jacob's peaceful loving eyes and how easily he had forgiven her, and what Danny had done no longer even registered in her heart. It didn't matter that he left her crying at the front door. She understood why. What was done couldn't be undone, and he had made it up to her a hundred times. The pain in her chest that she had been carrying simply evaporated.

'Oh my God, did you get a sneak peak on Jessie's patient? Totally hot.'

'The bike vs. car dude?'

'Yeah, the blond surfy with the impressive biceps.'

'Oh Bec, you're such a shocker. Yeah, he's all right, but not really my type. I don't go for the scruffy look. But I can see he's your type.' The two nurses giggled while they finished making her bed while she was still in it. *Yeah, totally humiliating, indeed.*

Who were they talking about? She willed open her eyes. She wanted to check out the 'bike vs. car dude' too, but they remained glued shut. She wondered what they nicknamed her.

She swallowed hard. Her voice box moved up and down freely; thank goodness, the annoying full feeling in her throat was gone. And thank goodness she was no longer lost in the dark void. That was a major relief.

The two nurses finished up and pulled back the curtains. 'All done, she looks nice and beautiful for your visit,' said one of them.

'Thanks. She does look better today, don't you think?' Daniel said as he entered the room.

'Sure does. She seems to have picked up since we disconnected the ventilator. They always look so much more like themselves when that comes off,' answered the nurse. 'Bet you're relieved to see it gone.'

'Totally, the less crap attached to her the better, I say.' She felt her hand being grabbed. 'Hey there Starlah, how are you today?' Daniel leaned down and kissed her forehead. She could feel his warm breath across her face. She scrunched her eyes.

'Whoa, did you see that? When I kissed her, her eyes fluttered,' he said excitedly.

'Won't be long, I reckon, and she'll open them for us,' the nurse said.

'God, I hope so.' He squeezed her hand hard.

'I'll leave you two alone. Call out if you need anything,' the nurse said.

'Thanks.'

'Okey dokey, enjoy your visit,' the nurse said as she walked out the door.

Starlah heard the door being closed and a chair being dragged across the floor and put next to the bed. She heard Danny sigh as he sat down in the chair and grabbed her hand again. He rubbed it with his thumb for a while.

He cleared his throat. 'So a lot's being going down since you … um,'—he cleared his throat again—'since *you know*. So I suppose I should keep you posted, but I don't want you worrying about it, OK?' He squeezed as though instilling an order.

'Well, that scumbag Brad has been officially charged with attempted murder, and a court date has been set for four months.' He leaned in and whispered, 'You'd be pleased to hear that my gig with Davo is squared up. I know I never told you the truth about that, and it breaks my heart—so wake the fuck up so I can explain, Starbright.' His voice cracked.

He took a deep breath. 'Anyway, you know how I was in the joint. Well, my cellie was one of the Zarburas, right? He had the gift of the gab and confessed a lot of shit to me about that bloody drug gig they had going.'

He leaned in closer and lowered his voice. 'Well, the cops gotta whiff of that shit, and they approached me with a deal. I'd get early release if I told them about what I knew.' He hesitated, then swallowed hard and continued.

'Turns out it wasn't enough to arrest the head guy. So the cops tell me I gotta step up and go undercover for them. I'm like no freaking way, I've got you and Sara to think about, but they said it was part of the early release deal and that I gotta follow through. Fuckin' cops …'

He sighed again and tenderly swiped her hair to the side. 'You look so peaceful, Starbright—it's freaking me out. Please wake up, Starlah,' he whispered close to her ear.

When she didn't respond he leaned back in the chair and sighed. After a while he continued, 'So I did what I had to. They've arrested a bunch of guys, and I'm free from any debts owed. Ain't that good?'

She smiled; she hoped it came out across her face. Danny was a good guy after all. She knew it. Now he was free to live his life without all that crap. She wanted to jump up and hug him and shout: *Danny, I'm so proud of you.*

She thought about Dave. Wow, Davo a cop, what a freak-out. That would explain the authoritarian vibe she got from him. She had to wake up to thank him for helping her. She needed him to know she was grateful.

Arthur waited for the nurse to leave before he tried getting up again. The previous nurse looking after him the other days wasn't on, so her orders of remaining in bed didn't count, he concluded. Something was calling him. He felt an overwhelming urge to get out of there. It wasn't a conscious thought. It was more instinctive, like his life depended on it.

He managed to manoeuvre himself out of bed more easily this time. His leg still throbbed but held his weight. He shuffled over to the wardrobe and looked inside for clothes that might belong to him. He found a pair of light blue denim shorts and a torn black T-shirt. He grabbed them and took them into the bathroom.

He ripped off the ID tags attached to his wrist and ankle, untied the gown and let it drop to the floor, and then he got dressed. He eyed himself in the mirror and frowned; he looked a mess. He turned the tap on and tried to clean the remaining dry blood out of his hair and across his face. He winced at the pain but didn't stop.

He reassessed himself in the mirror: much better. He cracked open the door and peered out towards the nurse's station—all clear. He made his way out of the room and into the corridor. He turned from side to side, wondering which direction he should go. He felt a strong pull to the left.

Walking that way felt life-affirming. He avoided eye contact with the passers-by and continued up the corridor. He seemed to be invisible. No one stopped him. The further up the corridor he went, the more his heart seemed to be responding to something.

He walked past room 23A and felt his heart beat erratically. He seemed to forget how to breathe. He stopped and backtracked a few paces and stood facing the room. He had to go inside. There was no other option. His mind wouldn't let him continue walking past.

He stepped through the door and pulled back the curtains. He gasped. She was so beautiful and looked so peaceful lying there. He remained silent just watching her, not wanting to disturb her. Did he know her? He wasn't sure, but he did feel drawn and connected to her. Who was she, and what happened to her?

He walked up to the bed. Her eyelids fluttered. The heart monitor attached to her alarmed. Her heart rate rocketed up to 165 bpm, and his responded in unison. A memory flashed through his mind. The two of them kissed and then burst into a violet and silver spinning flame. He went to clutch something around his neck. There wasn't anything there.

The curtain flew back, and an enraged man burst into the room. 'What the hell did you do to her?' He lunged at Arthur but then changed direction and raced towards the girl and clutched her hand.

Two nurses raced in. One went over to the girl; the other came over to him and ushered him out of the room. He didn't want to leave. He wanted to stay with her but allowed himself to be led out.

'Who is she?' Arthur stared over the nurse's shoulder towards the unconscious woman. He wanted and needed to be with her. The beauty of her flawless skin, the way her golden hair fanned out around her head and the way her pouty lips mesmerised him all pulled at his heart.

'Listen, you need to leave, or I'm going to have to get security to escort you back to bed.' The head nurse had her hand against his chest, pushing him out of the room. Then she closed the door behind her and leaned against it, blocking his way.

She looked intent and scary. Arthur understood now why his nurse seemed to tiptoe around her. He backed away. There was no point in challenging her, considering he didn't even know who the woman was, and he knew he wasn't exactly being rational.

He reluctantly turned away and kept walking. He needed to get away from the craziness of this place and the crazy effect this stranger had on him.

THIRTY-SIX

WHAT THE hell was that freak doing in here? Seriously, where the hell is your security guy? Fuck, man, do you guys just let any weirdo walk into people's room? What if Brad had an accomplice and sent that freak to finish her off? Fuck!' Daniel paced around her bed. She could hear him breathing fast. She imagined he would be running his hand through his hair.

She tried to open her mouth. She felt as though she was underwater and was about to break through to the surface. She was almost there. *Don't worry Danny, everything is all right.*

But who was that man? She sensed he belonged with her. He wasn't there to do her harm. He was someone she knew … somehow. Her body recognised him; her heart most definitely did.

She had to break through to the surface, she just had to. She willed her eyes open. They still resisted. *Please, please let me wake up.* She concentrated on her brain. If she could just wake up then Daniel would know she was all right, and she could tell him to race after that man and get him back. She needed to know who he was.

'Please calm down, Mr Rose. I'm truly sorry, but I don't think he meant her any harm. He is one of our head injury patients. They sometimes get confused and disorientated, that's all.' The nurse tried to reassure him.

'Yeah well, you guys should be more vigilant of your patients' movements,' he answered tersely. He took a few deep breaths and tried to calm himself down. 'Sorry, I'm still freaked out. I know it's not your fault.'

He went over to Starlah's bed and grabbed her hand with one hand. With the other he stroked her hair. 'It's fine. You can go now. She seems to be all right,' he told the nurse.

'Very well—and again I'm sorry our patient scared you.' She turned and walked away.

'Hey Starlah, what's going on in there? Come on, time to wake up,' he said as he leaned down and kissed her on the forehead. He waited to see if there was any response, and then continued. 'Oh, I almost forgot. The cops found your pendant at the house, and I've got it right here.' He reached over and clipped it around her neck. 'There, that looks better, hey?'

She felt the familiar comfort of it, but there was something missing. She wasn't really sure what, but somehow she had a feeling that the pendant meant so much more to her than a simple piece of jewellery. On the outskirts of her consciousness she heard a whisper, but she couldn't make it out.

Arthur walked as fast as his legs would allow. He couldn't get her image out of his mind. Why did she have that effect on him? He shook his head and kept focused on getting out of there. He kept his head down as he walked. What was it about her lips that spoke to him, despite making no sound?

Aargh … get out of my head, he ordered. He bumped into someone. 'Sorry,' he said as he kept walking.

'Hey, why are you out of bed? Arthur, come back here,' the doctor yelled out.

Arthur moved faster. The front door was only metres away. He had to get away from them all. He walked through the door, half-expecting the security guard to tackle him. He looked over his shoulder, but it didn't seem that anyone was following him. Good.

He made his way through a group of people waiting for the bus and headed north. It was as good as any other direction, considering he had no destination. His legs still felt new to him, as though he was a newborn learning to walk. He kept his head down and concentrated on moving one step at a time.

He shoved his hands into his pocket, and his left hand felt something cool. He pulled it out and stopped. It was a crystal pendant shaped into a flame. It was the first thing that felt familiar to him, but why?

He put it over his head and felt an electric charge travel through his body, causing him to waver and lose his breath. It heated up his whole being. It pulsed and felt like it crackled through every nerve ending, searing them with information, unveiling the cloud blocking his memories.

Then it hit him. 'Starlah …' He turned back the way he came and ran.

Starlah finally burst through the surface of the water and gasped. She clutched at the pendant. There was only one word on her lips, the one word that meant it all, *Ardaleigh*.

Ardaleigh burst through the door breathlessly. Daniel jumped to his feet and stared at the stranger, then at Starlah.

Starlah squinted and tried to raise her head. Her eyes had trouble focusing. She could see a figure standing at the door. He seemed familiar, yet she didn't recognise him. 'Ardaleigh?' she croaked blinking her eyes repetitively. 'Is that you?' she asked hoping, praying that somehow it could be.

He grinned, walking into the sterile-smelling hospital room. He approached tentatively, eyeing Daniel, then Starlah. 'Yes, it's me. I finally made it,' he said. He stopped at the foot of the bed and waved his hand up and down in front of him. 'Um, sorry about my new look.'

She blinked hard. 'I don't understand. What's happening?'

He stared down at his dishevelled foreign body and shrugged. 'Well, I'm here now, and this is me.' He waved his hand in front of him again, attempting to only disclose enough to trigger her awareness. His face, still swollen and bruised, looked uncomfortable and unsure of himself. He held his breath, awaiting her response.

She stared at his pendant, and a faint smile spread across her dry lips. She reached her hand out as a tear rolled down her cheek. 'Mm—different.'

He grabbed her hand and kissed the top of it. 'You can thank Katalin for that, or you'd be babysitting me instead.' His eyes filled with tears.

Daniel stood there shaking his head. 'Will someone please tell me what the fuck is going on?'

They both turned and looked at him. Their cheeks infused with heat. Starlah reached her other hand with the cast on it out and beckoned to him. 'Oh Danny, I'm so sorry about everything.' She couldn't remember a lot of what led her to this point, but she knew it must have caused him a great deal of heartache. She darted her eyes back to Ardaleigh and then Daniel. *Oh God, what must this look like to poor Danny?* 'Um, this is Ardaleigh …'

'It's Arthur Snow while we're here.' He shrugged self-consciously and darted his eyes towards the hallway.

'Arthur Snow? Well, don't expect me to call you that outside these walls.' She tried to smile at him, but a pain across her skull caused her to suck in a deep breath.

Daniel rushed over. A dazed look played across his concerned features as he grabbed her hand while darting his eyes back and forth between the weird guy standing next to his sister and her pale face. He looked down at her again, 'God, are you OK?

Shit, you're awake … Oh my God, you're actually awake.' He continued to stare at her, then at Ardaleigh as he stroked her hand.

Starlah pushed down the pain and smiled. She was glad she made it back. The look of relief on his face enlivened her heart. All the time he had spent by her bedside holding her hand, soothing her with his words helped bring her closer to the surface, and with the aid of Ardaleigh's presence and the pendant's energy she was able to make it back to them.

She looked at Ardaleigh, and her heart literally skipped a beat. She never really knew what that saying meant until this very moment. Staring into his eyes, even though they came in a different package, she completely understood its poetic significance. She closed her eyes and let out a steady breath. The two most important people in her life held her hands, and in this moment nothing else mattered.

TOMACE PACED around the room. In the solitude of his domain he allowed himself to indulge in his true feelings. He was enraged. Not only had Ardaleigh succeeded in being reunited with Starlah, but Katalin, his own twin flame had betrayed him.

He couldn't face looking Katalin in the eyes without his true feelings betraying him, so he stayed away from her. He would have to deal with her soon, but for now he was relieved she had to face the other Elders and answer their probing questions. He had some time to think.

Why did she do that? Why did she risk rebirth for the sake of *him*?

He gritted his teeth. He acknowledged that he should be beyond these emotions, and in his head he knew he risked being thrown out of the Elders' council. But he couldn't deny what was coursing through his heart. All he could think about was getting even with Ardaleigh.

The front door opened, and he spun around to face her tired chastened face. His heart sank. What was the consequence of her manipulation of the birthing process? He feared it may mean her being expelled from the Elders' Council.

'Greetings Katalin.' He hesitated before walking over to her. She kept her eyes lowered, but he could tell she had been crying.

'Tomace, please do not be disappointed in me.' She stood in the doorway, unsure of his reaction.

He had to fight hard not to grit his teeth. 'I am not disappointed, Katalin …' He had to turn away. He couldn't bear to have her look at him when he tried to lie to her.

'Tomace?' she gasped. 'Am I reading fury in your aura? I … I do not understand. Tell me this isn't so.' She walked around his back so she could look him in the face.

He gave in and clenched his jaw tight as he inhaled deeply with his eyes squeezed shut. He felt completely exhausted fighting himself and couldn't hold it in anymore. 'Yes, Katalin— my love. You do remember that, don't you?'

She cringed and grabbed her pendant.

'You do remember that I am your twin flame and your loyalty should lay in our bond. Not with him.' He snapped open his eyes and glared at her.

She stumbled backwards and gasped. 'I cannot believe what I am seeing. What has happened to you, my love?' She trembled.

He registered the shock and fear across her face and tried to regain control of his emotions. It was too late. Maybe in the

Third Realm he could have deceived her, but not here. He sighed and sank down onto a carved wooden chair.

'Katalin, I have failed you. I know you believed in me and that I was ready for ascension, but'—he dropped his face into his hand—'it seems we both may have been mistaken.' He looked up piteously.

'I have tried with all of my heart, but when I saw you were willing to sacrifice yourself for the sake of Ardaleigh, something ancient and primal boiled forth from my being.' He gritted his teeth again and shook his head hard. 'Why—why would you turn to him like that? Why would you show so much love and compassion for him?' He looked down at his clenched fists.

'I am your twin flame, not him,' he whispered, as he pinched the bridge of his nose and fought back tears. 'Sometimes I wonder what kind of bond your last two lives in the Third Realm together has forged.'

Katalin stared through her tears and swallowed hard. 'I think you are right. I think you have allowed yourself to indulge in many unevolved emotions.' She blinked, and tears cascaded down her cheeks.

'Jealously and anger?' She shook her head, 'Why do you choose to descend back there?' She turned and wiped at her tears. 'How many lives have we found ourselves in this exact moment of unfounded jealously and unevolved primal ownership and anger?'

She spun back around and glared at him. 'Very well, if we are being brutally honest then yes, I have fond affections for Ardaleigh, but not in a way that betrays our love. I love him as a mother would a child. Spending several lifetimes as his Earth mother I have retained some of those feelings and affections.' She clutched her pendant. 'And I wish ...'

He stared at her flushed face and felt a deep pain wracking his chest. 'What? What do you wish? Just say it.' He held his breath, fearing the worst. He had spent enough time as an Elder to know a few of their secrets. The one he feared the most was Katalin choosing to sever their twin flame bond. There were only a few chosen Elders who knew that was possible. He feared she was one of them.

'I wish you were more like Ardaleigh in your expressions of love,' she whispered as she sank down onto a chair opposite him. 'Tomace, I fear we have lost some of those things that make a twin flame love singular and exceptional. Ardaleigh would risk everything for his flame, and I fear you do not exhibit the same magnitude of love and sacrifice for our union.' She closed her eyes and heaved a sigh.

'When was the last time you even entertained taking me to the Chamber of Resonance to share our spiritual love or even to touch me with your hands and engage in a physical expression of our love?' Her face reddened.

He stared with his mouth gaping. She would dare to desire Ardaleigh's foolhardy ways of expressing love? It didn't even occur to him that she would need or desire these childish displays of affections. His understanding of what was expected of an Elder may have left him withdrawn and distant, and now he risked losing it all.

'Katalin, I am truly sorry. I have been so preoccupied in

controlling Ardaleigh and trying to modify his behaviour, I have allowed my own to go unobserved.' He went to her and rested his hand on her shoulder. 'But I do not see his total abandonment of self-control as a desirable way to show love.'

She placed her hand over his and allowed more tears to fall. 'I am afraid that your lack of self-monitoring has come with a price, my love. I fear it is beyond repair and we must go to the Elders and beseech their counsel.'

He pulled his hand free and stepped back. 'You would betray me again. But why?' He looked aghast. 'Why is it so easy for you to betray me, yet you were willing to give up everything to help him?'

She cast her eyes down. 'My love, your own words and heart betray you. I have a duty as a member of the council to seek their guidance in your confessions of your struggle with power, anger and jealousy. If I choose to hide the truth from the council then I too have failed. Maybe we both need another life through the Third Realm.' She looked back up into his eyes.

'You do understand why we must do this, don't you?' She clutched her pendant and searched his face. 'Ardaleigh's transgressions are love-based. Yours are more primal and not above reproach.'

He turned his back and pulled at his pendant until the chain snapped. He clutched it in his hand. So many thoughts and feelings bombarded his brain, but one still lingered foremost: he was going to get even with Ardaleigh.

ACKNOWLEDGEMENTS

WRITING IS such a solitary activity, yet without all the people behind the scene lending support, patience and advice it would not be a productive endeavour.

I'd sincerely like to thank all those people who in some way have enriched the writing of my debut novel. A massive, over-the-top thanks goes to Suzanne Kibble, whose belief makes magic happen. Naomi Brimson-Johnson thank you for your encouragement, enthusiasm and great feedback, and for taking the time to read my many revisions. I promise this IS the last version … your belief works magic too.

My editor, Kelly Hart; thanks for your great advice and amazing ability to see the raw beauty before the polish is applied.

Anthony at Book Cover Cafe, you totally rock the cover world; love your work.

And a huge, heartfelt, fluffy thank you to all the amazing authors from The Rainforest Writing Retreat, who entertain and enlighten my heart and mind. Thank you Charmaine Clancy, Kaz Delaney and Sheryl Gwyther, without your talented gifts I'm not sure if I would've found the courage.

And thanks to my readers, for taking the time to share in Starlah and Ardaleigh's world, I hope you enjoyed it as much as I enjoyed discovering and writing about it.

ABOUT THE AUTHOR

SUZANA JAMES divides her time between writing YA/New Adult paranormal fiction, nursing and being a mum.

She is a member of the Gold Coast Rainforest Writing Retreat, loves travelling and all shades of pink. She lives by the motto; a dash of pink a day, keeps the grumpy bums away.

Her year living amongst the Tibetan Buddhist society in the Himalayas has inspired her passion for delving into the deeper layers of the human psyche. Many of these concepts can been seen woven through her debut novel: *Melody's Stone*.